Re-imagined by Tim Burton

PLANET
OF THE APES

FOREWORD BY
RICHARD D. ZANUCK

INTRODUCTION BY
TIM BURTON

SCREENPLAY BY
WILLIAM BROYLES, JR. AND LAWRENCE KONNER & MARK D. ROSENTHAL

CONTRIBUTING WRITER MARK SALISBURY

PHOTOGRAPHS BY SAM EMERSON AND DAVID JAMES

EDITED BY DIANA LANDAU   DESIGNED BY TIMOTHY SHANER

First Edition

01   02   03   10   9   8   7   6   5   4   3   2   1

ISBN 1-55704-486-4 (paperback)   ISBN 1-55704-487-2 (hardcover)

Library of Congress Cataloguing-in-Publication Data is available on request.

QUANTITY PURCHASES
Companies, professional groups, clubs, and other organizations may qualify for special terms when ordering quantities of this title. For information, write Special Sales,
Newmarket Press, 18 East 48th Street, New York, NY 10017, call (212) 832-3575, fax
(212) 832-3629, or e-mail mailbox@newmarketpress.com.

www.newmarketpress.com

Manufactured in the United States of America

Other Newmarket Pictorial Moviebooks include:

contents

A Passion Reborn

By Richard D. Zanuck

IT was thirty-four years ago that my late friend, Arthur P. Jacobs, walked into my office at Twentieth Century Fox and told me the story that would become *Planet of the Apes*. I'd thought that Arthur, a well-respected public relations man, was coming in to talk about a client of his starring in one of our movies (I was head of the studio at the time). But instead Arthur told me about a book he had optioned—written by Pierre Boulle, author of *Bridge Over the River Kwai*—and wanted to make into a movie. The project, Arthur explained, origi-nally had been set up at Warner Bros., but they had put it into turnaround and now he was trying to revive it.

Arthur's passion was unmistakable. He came with not only a completed script but also a book filled with page after page of incredible conceptual drawings he had commissioned to illustrate his vision. To be frank, I didn't take Arthur's idea too seriously at first, but I liked him and admired the work of screen-writer Rod Serling, creator of the *Twilight Zone* TV series. So I took it home that weekend, read it in one sitting, and was instantly hooked. The basic idea, the concept of the

upside-down world, was instantly compelling. I was intrigued by the parallels the story drew between ape and man, by the rever-sal of power, and by the idea that the stronger of the species, not necessarily the more intelligent, was the one in control, with man as the downtrodden. It was great material for a movie. The next week I called Arthur into my office and we made a deal.

While Arthur went on to produce all five *Planet of the Apes* films, I left Fox soon after the second movie was released to continue my career as an independent producer. Through the years, it was always in the back of my mind that the idea which sparked this movie franchise could be reignited for today's audiences, but I never did anything about it. So when I read in

the Hollywood trade papers early in 2000 that Tim Burton had signed on to direct a new version for Fox, I was tempted to reach for the phone and offer my services as producer. Something stopped me, however. Tim was the ideal choice to direct this story, and I felt that some producer must be attached to the project already. Still, I didn't call. A couple of days later, totally out of the blue, Tom Rothman, then presi-dent of production at Fox, telephoned and invited me on board. Obviously I was thrilled and I will always be grateful to Tom for that call. While in some ways working on the new film has been like enter-ing my own time warp, the last year or so has been a truly wonderful experience—thanks to Tim Burton.

I didn't know Tim before we started but had always respected and admired his work. Now, having worked so closely with him, I know Tim to be that rare commod-ity: both an authentic genius and a wonderful human being. Every day would bring its own surprises as Tim re-imagined a new *Planet of the Apes* through his own unique vision. On set, he would turn what was written on the page into moments of pure brilliance. And yet he is also extremely collab-orative and open to suggestions. The crew loves him, the actors love him, I love him. I've worked with some talented, creative, passionate, and visionary directors through the years, but Tim is unsurpassed. Working with him on this film has been among the most creatively stimulating and rewarding experiences of my career. And I've no doubt that the enthusiasm, passion, and excitement we felt during the filming has made *Planet of the Apes* a spectacular and special film experience for audiences around the world.

ABOVE: Richard D. Zanuck, right, and Mark Wahlberg on the set of the 2001 production of *Planet of the Apes*. OPPOSITE: On the Lake Powell set of the original 1968 production.

mythmaking on screen

by Tim Burton

PLANET *of the Apes* tells a story that has become deeply ingrained in popular culture—it's a truly original, modern-day fairy tale that connects with audiences on so many levels. The opportunity to revisit this world, thirty-three years after the release of the original *Planet of the Apes* movie, really excited me. So many aspects of the original film and its four sequels were appealing—not least the scope of the mythology and the unique perspective and commentary the series provided on our own society.

The most challenging aspect of creating this new film was to be completely respectful of the mythology of the original, while adding new characters and story elements. I wasn't interested in creating a sequel or a remake. It was very important to me to keep the essence of the original present in this re-imagining. What I liked most about the screenplay was the character-driven nature of the story, as well as the extremely varied environments through which our characters would travel. *Planet of the Apes* is a world of contrasts—from the vacuum of space to the lush greens of the jungle to the vastness of the desert. These settings made a perfect stage for our astronaut, Leo Davidson, to face a shocking reversal of his own origins on a planet ruled by apes.

Another crucial step in our preparation was to make sure our talented actors would be able to act through the extensive makeup they would be required to endure. The gifted Rick Baker, whom I worked with before on *Ed Wood*, has truly pushed the boundaries of cinematic makeup once again. His brilliant team of artists and technicians created apes who were totally believable—on and offscreen.

Creating a movie on this scale is a tremendous challenge and would not have been possible without the passion and enthusiasm of the talented cast and crew who helped bring such a rich world to life. My special thanks go to production designer Rick Heinrichs, costume designer Colleen Atwood, cinematographer Philippe Rousselot, and composer Danny Elfman, and, of course, to producer Richard Zanuck, who brings a unique history to this project. They and countless others have helped us rediscover the strange and mystical *Planet of the Apes*.

FAR LEFT: Tim Burton's original ape concepts in watercolor. BACKGROUND: Guy Hendrix Dyas's pencil illustration of the ape effigy. RIGHT: Tim Burton on set.

"Take your **stinking paws** off me, you damned **dirty ape!**"

Charlton Heston in the original
Planet of the Apes, 1968

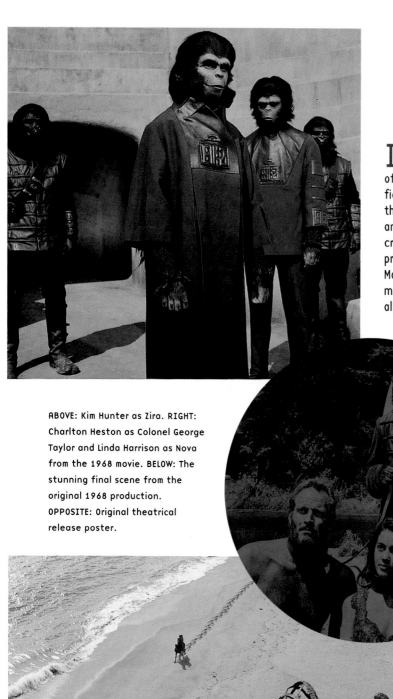

ABOVE: Kim Hunter as Zira. RIGHT: Charlton Heston as Colonel George Taylor and Linda Harrison as Nova from the 1968 movie. BELOW: The stunning final scene from the original 1968 production. OPPOSITE: Original theatrical release poster.

IN 1968 movie audiences got their first glimpse of a strange new world—one that would forever alter the landscape of cinema. *Planet of the Apes*, based on an acclaimed science fiction novel by Pierre Boulle (written in 1963), told the story of three American astronauts whose spaceship enters a time warp and is propelled three thousand years into the future, where it crash-lands on an unnamed planet—a planet on which man is a primitive beast dominated by intellectually superior apes. Moreover, apes that talk. And ride horses. And carry guns. And make the rules. A world where humans were not only intellectually but physically inferior, a weak, mute species, experimented on and treated as vermin.

Thrust into this hostile, topsy-turvy world were astronauts Taylor (Charlton Heston), Landon (Robert Gunner), and Dodge (Jeff Burton). After their ship goes down in a lake, the trio treks across a desert wilderness in search of food, finally encountering a group of people scavenging for corn and fruit. Before they can question them, a horde of gun-toting gorillas comes charging out of the trees on horseback, hunting down the humans and forcibly rounding up any survivors. Dodge is killed in the ensuing chaos, while Taylor is shot in the throat, an injury that (usefully in plot terms) renders him temporarily speechless.

Taken to a city run entirely by apes, Taylor is imprisoned. Although voiceless, he tries to communicate with his simian captors, who dismiss his protestations as the ravings of a "sub-simian" fool. Eventually he is befriended by a pair of sympathetic chimpanzees, scientist Zira (Kim Hunter) and her archaeologist husband Cornelius (Roddy McDowell), along with a savage human beauty, Nova, played by model Linda Harrison. When they discover Taylor can both speak and reason intelligently, Zira and Cornelius postulate that he could well be the missing link between the unevolved primate and higher apes. But the ruling orangutan politicians consider him a threat to apekind and schedule him for experimental cranial

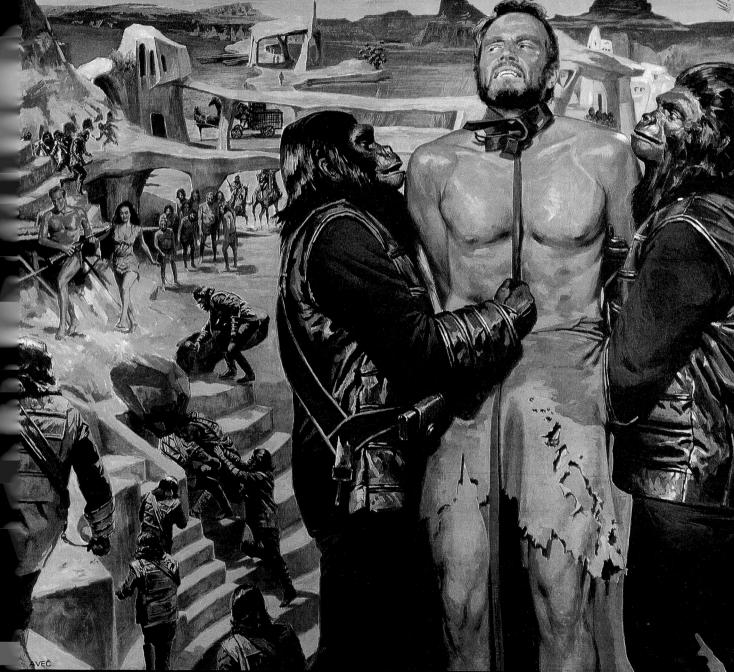

surgery. With the aid of Zira and Cornelius, Taylor and Nova escape into the Forbidden Zone, an uncharted land from which apes are prohibited, in an attempt to prove that intelligent humankind existed before simian-kind.

Masterfully directed by Franklin J. Schaffner—who would go on to direct the Oscar-winning *Patton*—from a screenplay co-written by *Twilight Zone* creator Rod Serling, *Planet of the Apes* was a huge commercial and critical success. It appealed both to young children, who were thrilled by the fantasy and talking apes, and adults who also enjoyed the spectacle but understood the film's pointed observations about the human predicament. The film's content tapped into the social and political climate of the time: flashpoint issues like Vietnam, civil rights, the Cold War, and the nuclear threat. "We were living in the traumatic sixties," recalls Linda Harrison, who played Nova in the 1968 film. "We had a really great fear of blowing up the planet. It was at a time when at school they'd teach you to get under the desk in case of a nuclear attack. So it struck at legitimate fears. And also the civil rights issues: the film communicated this division, the barriers that we'd built up. We were reflecting our own consciousness at the time."

Richard Zanuck, then head of production at Twentieth Century Fox as well as the studio head, had long championed the project. But even he wasn't too sure exactly how the public would react to the film and worried they might laugh at its talking apes. In fact, Zanuck says, it wasn't until after the first preview in Phoenix, Arizona, that he knew his decision to make the movie had been justified, and that the film worked with audiences. "Not until that instant did we realize that we had struck some kind of primal chord," he remembers. "People were absorbed by it. They liked the parallels we had drawn between ape and man. They were interested in the juxtaposition

of power it presented: the big 'what if?' If the world was turned around and you walk into this nightmare where everything is just reversed, and the stronger of the species is actually the one that's in control. You may have more intelligence, but you're helpless. You're the downtrodden, you're the minority. People were captivated by it."

And in particular by its downbeat denouement, in which Heston's astronaut Taylor and Harrison's Nova rode off together down a beach, farther into the Forbidden Zone, only to discover the half-buried remains of the Statue of Liberty protruding from the sand. The moment proved shattering for Taylor and audiences alike. The implication was simple: the planet Taylor had landed on was, in fact, Earth. He had been home all along. Mankind had all but annihilated itself in a nuclear Armageddon. Even today, thirty-three years later, the climax retains its chilling force.

Planet of the Apes became a cinematic and cultural phenomenon, and Twentieth Century Fox immediately began work on a sequel. *Beneath the Planet of the Apes*, released in 1970, starred James Franciscus as Brent, the leader of a rescue mission sent into space in search of Taylor and his crew. Heston himself appeared briefly, as did Linda Harrison, and the series went on to spawn another three movies—*Escape from the Planet of the Apes* (1971), *Conquest of the Planet of the Apes* (1972), and *Battle for the Planet of the Apes* (1973)—as well as a live action TV series and a cartoon show. Although the last movie was released in 1973, *Planet of the Apes*'s popularity has continued to grow, with generations of fans around the world hoping to return to the Planet one day.

ABOVE: Poster for the 1974 movie marathon, in which all five *Planet of the Apes* films were shown in one sitting. Courtesy Brian Penikas, apemania.com
LEFT: Original poster from the French theatrical release.

15

Re-imagining a Legend

THE prospect of returning to the *Planet of the Apes* had been contemplated by executives at Twentieth Century Fox for almost a decade. Various scripts had been commissioned, and a number of top-name directors had, at one time or another, been associated with the project. But it was not until the spring of 2000 that the idea became a reality. Armed with a new screenplay by *Apollo 13* scribe William Broyles, Jr., Fox's then-president of production Tom Rothman sought out Tim Burton, fresh from the success of *Sleepy Hollow*, to be the film's director. Although Burton was a huge fan of the original movie, he admits he wasn't sure initially about the need or wisdom of mounting a new *Planet of the Apes*.

"When I was first approached, I thought, oh, they're going to do a remake," says Burton, "which was not a good idea because it was such a good movie to begin with. I probably resisted wanting to do it because I subscribe to the idea that you don't remake great movies. I mean, remake a bad movie. When I look at the original *Planet*, I'm still personally entertained. I think it was way ahead of its time."

But Fox was determined that this new *Planet of the Apes* would not be a remake as such. Nor should it be thought of as a sequel but rather a "re-imagining" of the 1968 classic. "It's not a remake, because we did a pretty good job at the time with the first film," insists Richard Zanuck. "It still holds up, and we don't want to just repeat ourselves. It's an extension of the original idea: a world dominated by apes, and these apes are also smart. Maybe not as smart as you but certainly stronger. And you are the outcast, fighting for your rights. We've built the picture around that basic thesis. And I hope we'll tap into the same curiosity about the relationship between man and ape."

Burton well remembers seeing *Planet of the Apes* for the first time. "I was terrified of Charlton Heston," he laughs. "This was true of all of his films. I liked him for that, because he was so serious and intense that he made the story believable at that time in my life. But it was also the film's overall vibe—the shock, the purity, the advancements in the makeup. The Rod Serling script. It had the magic great movies have."

ABOVE: The 2001 theatrical release teaser poster. LEFT: Tim Burton's advancing ape army.

07.27.01
RULE THE PLANET.

Despite his initial reservations about revisiting the material, Burton found himself drawn to the themes of reversal, of an outsider thrust into an alien landscape—a motif that echoes throughout his work. "I got very intrigued by the idea of re-imagining this world," says Burton. "I was very affected by the story the first time around, and it stuck with me, like a good myth or fairy tale. Here's a movie that is so strong and still ahead of its time, with its own juice and dynamic."

"It does play well, but it's dated," muses Helena Bonham Carter, one of the stars of the new *Planet of the Apes*, who only recently caught up with the original. "And I thought, thank God, because then we're justified in redoing it. That film was so much of its time. Quite apart from the limits of the ape makeup, you've got Charlton Heston, and he's so super-macho that it's hilarious. Tim sees things from a very different point of view and has such a hilariously dark sense of humor, so this film will be funny in a different way."

With Burton on board as director, Fox needed a producer who would complement his unique artistic vision and help bring it and the film to fruition. That man was Richard Zanuck. Not only had Zanuck been in charge of Twentieth Century Fox when the first two *Planet of the Apes* were made, but also he had taken a very hands-on approach in the production of the original. Since leaving Fox, Zanuck, whose family name is legendary in Hollywood, had carved out a career as a highly respected and hugely successful independent producer whose credits include *Jaws*, *The Sting*, and *Driving Miss Daisy* among many others. For Zanuck, the opportunity to return to the *Planet of the Apes* was a dream come true.

"During my nine years at Fox, we made more than a hundred pictures and some great ones, too, like *Patton*, *M*A*S*H*, *Butch Cassidy*, and *The French Connection*," Zanuck recalls. "But of all of the films I made in those years, this is the only one I would have been interested in revisiting as a producer, because I think it has somewhere to go. And I think we can do it better. With advances in makeup and effects, we can create a sense of reality that we didn't have before. People bought it because it was the first time they'd seen anything like it. Now they're more sophisticated."

the passion of Tim Burton

"WHEN you say *Planet of the Apes* and Tim Burton in the same breath, that idea is instantly explosive, like lightning on the screen," says producer Richard Zanuck. Adds executive producer Ralph Winter, "We're making Tim Burton's *Planet of the Apes*, and you're going to see that in every bit of design, from wardrobe to makeup to the sets and the action, the characters, all the layers Tim brings to it."

Tim Burton is one of the great cinematic visionaries. Since making his feature directorial debut in 1985 with the hilariously subversive comedy *Pee-Wee's Big Adventure*, he has continued to bring his decidedly personal vision to the screen in films of enormous imagination and artistic dexterity, fusing extraordinary production design and dazzling visual wit with soul-searching performances. Burton entered the industry as an animator at Walt Disney in the late 1970s and has operated within the Hollywood studio system ever since, while managing to maintain his artistic independence. Not only are Burton's films beautifully crafted, each also contains a deeply personal core fueled by emotion, symbolism, and sometimes his own inner torment. His characters invariably are misunderstood outsiders who operate on the fringes of their society, tolerated but pretty much left to their own devices. Much like Burton himself, in fact. "My movies sort of ended up being representative of the way I am," he once said.

Consequently Burton's work has remained as refreshingly idiosyncratic as his very first film, the five-minute stop-motion short *Vincent*. From the spooky afterlife comedy *Beetlejuice*, a tour de force of imaginative design and outré special effects, to his blockbusting gothic reinterpretations of the Batman mythology in *Batman* and *Batman Returns*; from his touching modern-day fable *Edward Scissorhands* to the manic energy of his alien invasion comedy *Mars Attacks!*; from the sweetly sensitive biopic *Ed Wood* to the animated musical extravaganza *The Nightmare Before Christmas*, which he produced from his own story, Burton's films have largely found a home with movie critics and the public alike, making him one of

ABOVE: Storyboard panel by Michael Jackson. CENTER: Tim Burton reviews the script with Helena Bonham Carter (Ari), left, and Tim Roth (Thade). BELOW: A Mauro Borelli concept drawing of Ape City. FAR RIGHT: Burton on the jungle set.

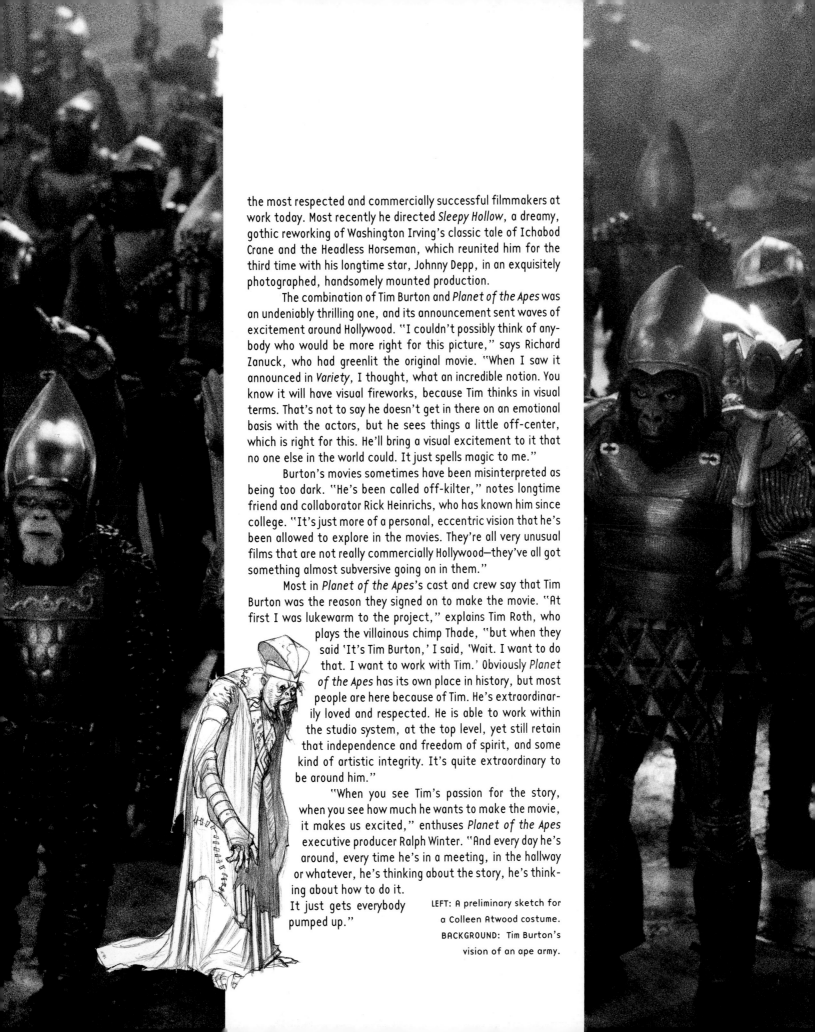

the most respected and commercially successful filmmakers at work today. Most recently he directed *Sleepy Hollow*, a dreamy, gothic reworking of Washington Irving's classic tale of Ichabod Crane and the Headless Horseman, which reunited him for the third time with his longtime star, Johnny Depp, in an exquisitely photographed, handsomely mounted production.

The combination of Tim Burton and *Planet of the Apes* was an undeniably thrilling one, and its announcement sent waves of excitement around Hollywood. "I couldn't possibly think of anybody who would be more right for this picture," says Richard Zanuck, who had greenlit the original movie. "When I saw it announced in *Variety*, I thought, what an incredible notion. You know it will have visual fireworks, because Tim thinks in visual terms. That's not to say he doesn't get in there on an emotional basis with the actors, but he sees things a little off-center, which is right for this. He'll bring a visual excitement to it that no one else in the world could. It just spells magic to me."

Burton's movies sometimes have been misinterpreted as being too dark. "He's been called off-kilter," notes longtime friend and collaborator Rick Heinrichs, who has known him since college. "It's just more of a personal, eccentric vision that he's been allowed to explore in the movies. They're all very unusual films that are not really commercially Hollywood—they've all got something almost subversive going on in them."

Most in *Planet of the Apes*'s cast and crew say that Tim Burton was the reason they signed on to make the movie. "At first I was lukewarm to the project," explains Tim Roth, who plays the villainous chimp Thade, "but when they said 'It's Tim Burton,' I said, 'Wait. I want to do that. I want to work with Tim.' Obviously *Planet of the Apes* has its own place in history, but most people are here because of Tim. He's extraordinarily loved and respected. He is able to work within the studio system, at the top level, yet still retain that independence and freedom of spirit, and some kind of artistic integrity. It's quite extraordinary to be around him."

"When you see Tim's passion for the story, when you see how much he wants to make the movie, it makes us excited," enthuses *Planet of the Apes* executive producer Ralph Winter. "And every day he's around, every time he's in a meeting, in the hallway or whatever, he's thinking about the story, he's thinking about how to do it. It just gets everybody pumped up."

LEFT: A preliminary sketch for a Colleen Atwood costume.
BACKGROUND: Tim Burton's vision of an ape army.

storycrafting

WITH both director and producer in place, attention focused on refining and sharpening the story and screenplay, which, like the first film, featured an astronaut crash-landing on a planet ruled by apes. The latest writer to tackle the script had been William Broyles, Jr., a former journalist and *Newsweek* editor who had turned to screenwriting with much success, writing or co-writing scripts for such hit movies as *Apollo 13*, *Entrapment*, and *Cast Away*.

Broyles had decided not to set his version of *Planet of the Apes* on Earth, as was the case with the original film, but on a different planet altogether, called Ashlar, because he "wanted to remove the thought that this is a repetition of the first movie." To that end, Broyles also threw out the original film's cynical human hero, Taylor, a character so embittered and disenchanted with mankind that he literally leaves the Earth, and whose entire philosophy was perhaps summed up in his line, "Somewhere in this universe there must be something better than man." The new lead, Leo Davidson, was on a "journey of self-discovery," says Broyles, "which to me is more interesting. Someone who's not completely formed yet, looking to find his destiny." Like Taylor before him, Davidson was an astronaut but was younger and "more capable of change."

As with the original movie, Broyles saw his *Planet of the Apes* as a way to impart social and political truths. "I thought it was a way to really get into the heart of humanity," he explains, "who we are and ideas of acceptance and tolerance and prejudice. I think you can deal with those themes very effectively in a science fiction setting. What can we learn in an upside-down world where apes are the species in charge? Ultimately this story is about the value of consciousness and decency, whether possessed by a human or an ape, because extremists of both species are interested in treating the other species as beneath contempt. The essence of these movies is to lay bare the prejudice among humans toward each other. If at the same time it raises consciousness about our primate cousins, that's great too."

Integral to Broyles's plot was the relationship between the human astronaut, Leo Davidson (played by Mark Wahlberg), and Ari (Helena Bonham Carter), a female chimpanzee. Unlike Kim Hunter's Zira in the original movie, whose interest in Taylor was "more academic and intellectual," Ari's interest in Davidson would be "much more passionate, less restrained," Broyles decided. This created an underlying sexual tension between the two that wasn't apparent in the original film. "If you accept that consciousness goes across species—that there's some moral core whether you're ape or human—then ultimately what attracts is the individual's heart more than their appearance."

Broyles feels that the film "has to do with a sense of possibility, of adventure, of making a difference. A lot of people feel cut off from any larger purpose, trapped in their own little world. This speaks to the value of heart, of putting yourself on the line for what's important. Our world is divided in so many ways, and I hope this makes us look at people across cultural or racial or intellectual or national or religious divides, in a different way. Besides," he smiles, "it's a great adventure story."

As Zanuck and Burton began working with Broyles's script, which according to Zanuck was very science-fiction-based, the story began to change. "We worked with Bill until probably July," says executive producer Ralph Winter, "and then we felt it was time to get another take on it, help Tim feel that he's putting his stamp on it and taking it in his direction." Screenwriters Lawrence Konner and Mark D. Rosenthal, whose credits include *Mighty Joe Young*, *Mercury Rising*, and *Jewel of the Nile*, were then drafted onto the project to ready the script for a November start date. "It was very clear from the beginning that Tim wanted this to be an incredible visual experience," reveals Konner. "He talks in a way that often starts with the visual, and works out to the story from there. You're having what seems like a normal conversation about a normal story point, and then it becomes Tim Burton–ized and goes in a whole other direction."

"There's definitely been an attempt to make it fresh and different, to separate ourselves from the first movie," says Ralph Winter. "That's been a deliberate effort all along. It's not that we're unaware of what the first movie did, but we've tried to make this Tim's."

ABOVE CENTER AND OPPOSITE BACKGROUND: Many details reinforce the film's theme of reversal. OPPOSITE CENTER: Mark Wahlberg as Leo and Helena Bonham Carter as Ari share a moment.

While Konner and Rosenthal kept many of the same characters and situations that Broyles had invented, they pared down the story's science fiction content and condensed into one climactic conflict the three *Braveheart*-sized battle sequences between humans and apes that Broyles had sketched. "This is a very old-fashioned story," notes Konner. "It's a guy who comes to a place, sees that people are being mistreated, and feels he has to leave it a better place than he finds it."

As with the original, the movie has a subtext (for those who want one) in the subjugation of humans by the apes, who even keep children as pets. "It's a metaphor for that kind of mistreatment, the sense that some people are privileged and some aren't," Konner continues. "The humans are the oppressed underclass. They are hunted, they're captured and enslaved, they are forced to be domestics or work in mines and fields; they are given little food."

"You could equate it on one level to the importing of people from Africa into slavery," muses actor Tim Roth about the film's political and ethical implications. "My character is the head of the military, and he is for wiping the humans out, getting rid of them. The humans are just fodder to him. He finds them disgusting. They smell very strange. They don't groom. And to him they're monsters. But there's also a human rights movement going on in the ape world, represented by Helena Bonham Carter's character."

Burton was determined that, compared with the original, the behavior of the apes on his planet should be more ... well, apelike. "Part of the interest of this material is seeing ourselves, how we treat each other, how we treat animals, the flip sides of things," he says. "We'd been doing a lot of analysis of chimps and apes and wanted to try to interweave some of that into their characters and into the battle scenes. We have all seen battles before. But we wanted to give these apes a strength and agility of movement that we haven't seen in this material before."

"My partner, Mark, has a history with apes," Konner explains. "He's spent time in Borneo with orangutans and in Africa with gorillas, and so he was the one most focused on asking the question at each moment in the script: What would an ape do here? Of course, Tim is looking for a balance between ape and human behavior. They're not quite human, not quite ape, so we had to keep asking: Are we going too far in one direction or another? Tim's done a fantastic job of walking that line, being very clear about what he wants those apes to be, and making sure they're never too human or too apelike.

"Although the apes talk like humans, they often act in a much more animalistic way," Konner continues. "Their reaction is to act immediately and think about it later. So when you're writing, you're trying to imagine the most primitive, most powerful reaction you could have to a situation and write it from there. Then sometimes you need to put the governor on and bring it back a little bit more toward the human."

ABOVE: Executive Producer Ralph Winter with Producer Richard D. Zanuck on the Ape City set.
RIGHT: Thade, played by Tim Roth, shows his dark side.

The Right People in the Right Places

WITH Twentieth Century Fox aiming for a summer 2001 release date, Burton and Zanuck began assembling key production personnel as work continued on the script—then entitled *The Visitor*, a decoy moniker designed to throw journalists off the scent. Their partner from the start had been executive producer Ralph Winter. A veteran of four *Star Trek* movies, Winter, whose credits also include *Mighty Joe Young* and *Inspector Gadget*, had recently produced Bryan Singer's *X-Men* for Fox and was used to handling enormous and complex productions on extremely tight deadlines. "This is certainly the largest film I've ever worked on and probably a lot of the crew as well," Winter says. "The size of the makeup and wardrobe in this show is historic. The budget is huge. Probably the largest Fox has ever greenlighted."

Not only was the scale of the production hugely ambitious, but also Fox had to start shooting in early November to make its planned summer release date. With shooting scheduled to last through to early March 2001, this meant both a compressed preproduction period and an accelerated postproduction. From a logistical perspective, it required Winter to draw up a battle plan of almost military precision. "We're looking at around 750 people on payroll, and making up 500 apes. At times on location we'll be feeding well over a thousand people," he explains. "Manufacturing sets and pieces all over the world. Sending people out all over the world to find stuff, because there's just not enough time to make everything and bring it back in time to shoot."

To create *Planet of the Apes*'s simian cast, Burton called upon six-time Oscar-winning makeup artist Rick Baker, whose credits include *Men in Black, An American Werewolf in London, Gremlins 2, Harry and the Hendersons*, and *The Nutty Professor* among many others. One major requirement for the production was a massive makeup crew to create the ape makeups and then apply them on a daily basis throughout filming. "Our first pass at assembling the makeup and hair department was 170 people," Winter reveals. "When they shot the original *Planet*, it actually stopped other

ABOVE LEFT: Drawing by James Rama. ABOVE: Cinematographer Philippe Rousselot. LEFT: Makeup designer Rick Baker touching up actor David Warner, who plays Ari's father, Sandar. RIGHT: Costume designer Colleen Atwood prepares Attar for battle, played by Michael Clarke Duncan.

Rick Heinrichs won an Oscar for his work on *Sleepy Hollow;* composer Danny Elfman began his film career on *Pee-Wee's Big Adventure* and, except for *Ed Wood*, has scored every Burton film since. Costume designer Colleen Atwood has collaborated with Burton several times, and editor Chris Lebenzon has cut every film for Burton since *Batman Returns.* "It reminds me of working in music with Don Was," muses Kris Kristofferson, who plays one of the human inhabitants of Burton's *Planet,* "because he brings all his good people, and they're all like he is. They're nice, smart and know what they're doing."

One newcomer to the Burton camp was acclaimed French cinematographer Philippe Rousselot. An Oscar winner for his ravishingly beautiful photography on Robert Redford's *A River Runs Through It*, Rousselot also counts among his credits *The People vs. Larry Flynt, Interview with the Vampire,* and *Dangerous Liaisons.* "Philippe brings a wonderful sensibility to augment Tim's vision," Winter says. "We are so fortunate to have him. We're shooting this picture in anamorphic, and the lenses tend to be just a little bit slower, which traditionally means you need a little more light. But Philippe makes do with the least amount of equipment I've ever seen. It's astonishing. He's got a great crew and a great attitude. He's fun to be around."

productions in town because it took away so many makeup and hair people."

The downside of such large crews and shortened schedules is reflected in the movie's cost. "When I first read the script I thought it was a $150 million movie, and the studio didn't want to spend anywhere near that," notes Winter. His job was to "trim that down to a level that was responsible but that would still make the movie Tim wanted. Part of my job is giving Tim options. If you want to spend $100 million and shoot it in a day, we'll figure that out for you. You want to do something else, we'll figure that out. It's all about choices. But Tim is really good at working that stuff out. He's been around a long time. He knows how to make those accommodations."

Winter scoured the globe in search of suitable studio space to film *Planet of the Apes,* even toying with shooting the movie in Europe, but ultimately the location was dictated by the amount of crew Rick Baker would need to create the ape makeups. "It made more sense to be based in Los Angeles with Rick and his operation, which is unique in terms of its manufacturing capability," says Winter. In the end, the production based itself at the LA Center Studios in downtown Los Angeles, but also leased a soundstage at the Sony lot in Culver City. "We put a down payment on one of the biggest stages in Hollywood," Winter says. "We knew we were going to have a big set. We didn't know what it was going to be, but we got the biggest space we could find at the time."

Since Burton often works with many of the same production personnel time and again, his core creative crew on *Planet of the Apes* had a familiar feel. Production designer

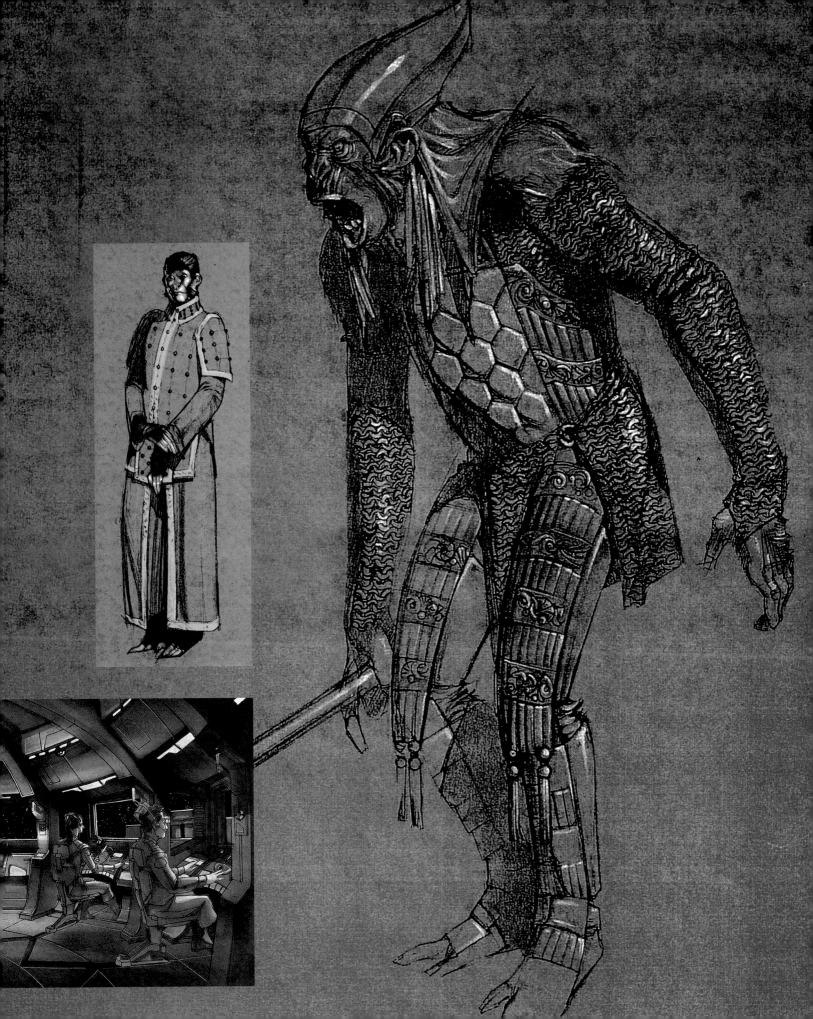

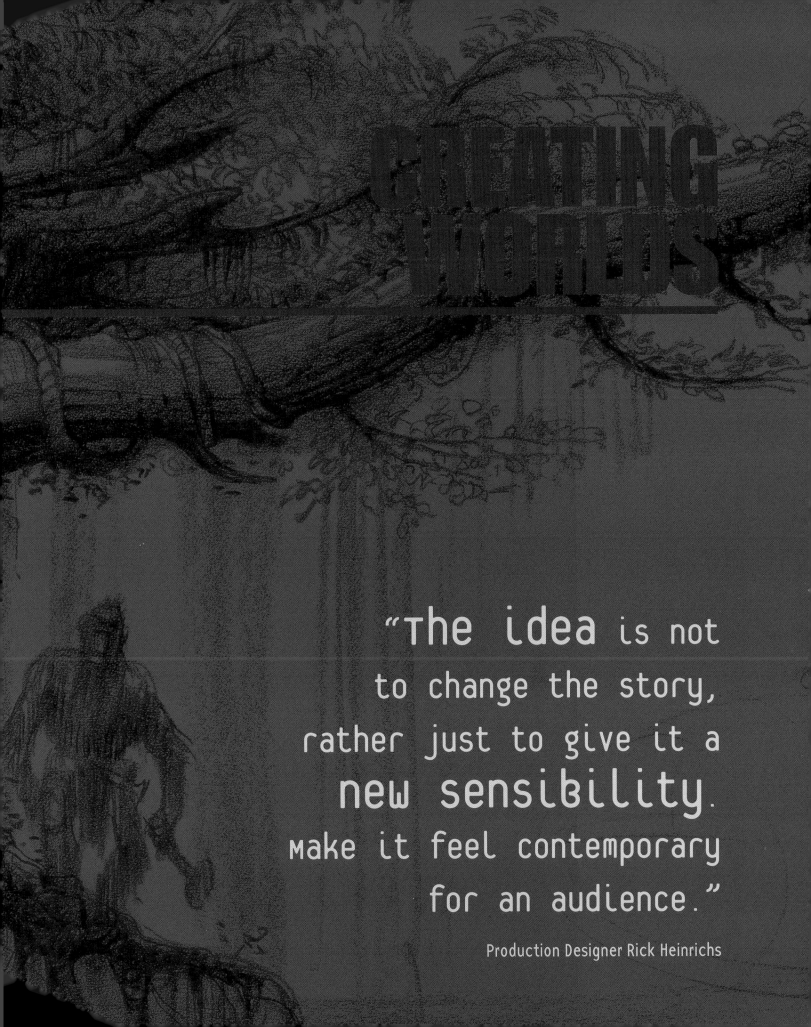

CREATING WORLDS

"The idea is not
to change the story,
rather just to give it a
new sensibility.
make it feel contemporary
for an audience."

Production Designer Rick Heinrichs

CHARGED with giving life to Burton's vision of *Planet of the Apes* was production designer Rick Heinrichs, whose relationship with the director dates back more than thirty years. The two first met while students at the California Institute for Arts. Both subsequently joined the animation department at Disney, where they collaborated on Burton's first directorial efforts, among them the stop-motion short *Vincent*. Heinrichs continued to work with Burton in a variety of capacities on *Batman Returns*, *Edward Scissorhands*, and *The Nightmare Before Christmas*, before embarking on a career as a production designer with the Coen brothers on *Fargo* and *The Big Lebowski*. He reteamed with Burton for his unrealized *Superman* project, before creating the amazing sets for *Sleepy Hollow*, which won him an Academy Award.

"When I first heard about the idea of doing *Planet of the Apes*, I think I had the same reaction a lot of people did: Why make it?" Heinrichs reflects. "It was so great the first time around. But, of course, Tim is always going to bring his own sensibility to it. It's very fertile ground for him. Tim's always enjoyed the dichotomy of animal–human behavior and the blending of the two. The question for us was,

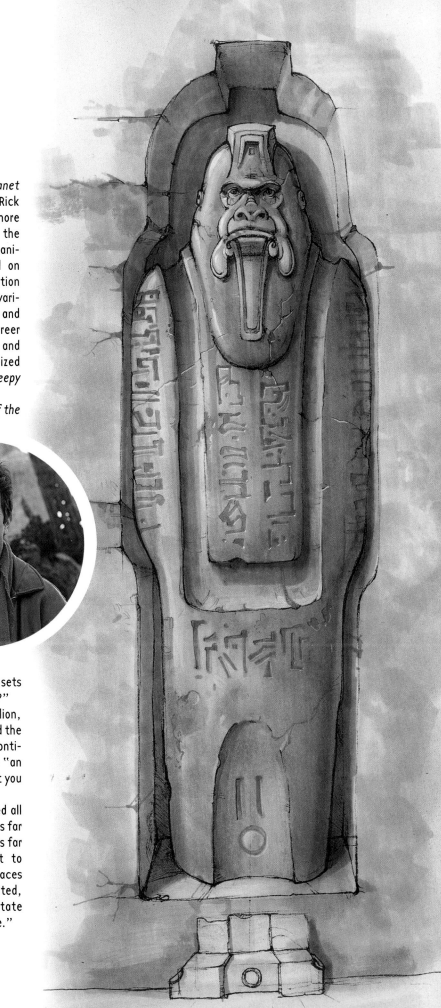

how do we show that visually? How do the sets create a background for that, and comment on it?"

Armed with a budget of between $11 and $12 million, Heinrichs began by asking himself: What kind of world would the apes occupy? He and Burton searched through several continents for suitably otherworldly places that would provide "an expansive view of the planet and a breadth and depth that you can only get on location."

"So we let Tim go," Ralph Winter notes. "We looked all over the world. We looked in Mexico, Central America, and as far north as parts of Canada. As far south as Chile. We went to Hawaii and a lot of other places to find the look Tim wanted, because that would dictate how we'd mount the movie."

LEFT: Early concept drawing by Sylvain Despretz of human slaves entering Ape City.
ABOVE: Rick Heinrichs.
RIGHT: James Oxford's concept drawing of an ape totem.

out of this world

THE production eventually settled on three very distinct main locations, one of which, the lava fields of Hawaii, would influence the film's entire look. "That was an early touchstone for us," Heinrichs explains. "We just loved the whole Saddle area of the Big Island of Hawaii and the vast fields of lava, and how the lava would flow and swirl around forested mountainous formations." This landscape, with islands of forested areas surrounded by vast stretches of arid "no-man's-land," allowed Heinrichs to establish the terrain of the planet in very simple, primordial terms. "That combination of terrains suggests a great conflict, and the competing bands of humans and apes are struggling with their own existence in a pretty harsh environment."

The second main location was Lake Powell, a manmade lake on the border of Utah and Arizona, where a number of scenes—including an attack on an ape encampment and the discovery of ape effigies—would be filmed. "Lake Powell provided us with the water that is key for some story elements, but also fantastic rock formations with no vegetation," Winter notes. "It's quite unusual to find water and rock formations without vegetation, and this is one of very few places on earth that suit our needs for this story." Although Lake Powell had been used as a location for the 1968 film, for the scenes of the spaceship crashing and the astronauts' trek across the desert, Heinrichs wasn't too concerned that the films would look alike. "Independence Bay, where we filmed, is a completely different area than was used for the original, so the look is different," he states. "It's a bizarre, otherworldly landscape. Since the lake was manmade, there was never meant to be a large body of water here, and the erosion is happening in an unnatural way so there's some fantastic formations. It proved to be a perfect environment—very beautiful, and a subtle nod to the original film."

"You really feel like you're on another planet when you're out there," agrees actor Mark Wahlberg. "I remembered it because I watched the original movie a couple of days before we went out there. But Tim really made it look different, and our location had its own distinct feel."

The third location chosen was the Trona Pinnacles, in the Mojave Desert near Ridgecrest, a three-hour drive from Los Angeles, where *Planet of the Apes*'s climactic battle sequence would be filmed. "A true alien landscape" is how Winter describes the pinnacles, a unique geological landscape consisting of more than 500 tufa (calcium carbonate) spires, some as high as 140 feet, spread over an area three miles wide by four and a half

RIGHT: The three main shooting locations from left to right: the lava fields of Hawaii, Lake Powell's Independence Bay, and the Trona Pinnacles in the Mojave Desert.

miles long. "Dry lakebeds that were underwater 20,000 years ago, bizarre formations that stick up out of the earth. It just captured Tim's imagination. I filmed there on *Star Trek V*, but since not many people saw that movie, it's sort of a virgin landscape. Tim has exploited the visual possibilities of this phenomenal place so it became a centerpoint of the movie's look."

"Each location has an interesting, otherworldly aspect to it," Heinrichs confirms. "We are trying to say: This is another world, and to leave doubt in the minds of the audience as to exactly where they are. Since the first movie did end up back on Earth, we want this not to feel earthbound."

As he did in Burton's *Sleepy Hollow*, Heinrichs decided to build as many sets as possible, creating both interiors and exteriors on stages that matched the locations chosen. This gave him optimum control of the filmed environments. "In all the movies I've worked on with Tim, there's something about the locations that will not be out of place when shot next to stage work," explains Heinrichs. "Usually it's something stylized about the natural environment. A lot of our locations are so bizarrely formed by nature and God, they occupy some kind of weird place between a location and a stage set."

Given their backgrounds in animation, Burton and Heinrichs approach design both graphically and sculpturally. "One of the things we always try to find is a two-dimensional graphic quality to the images, along with a very sculptural, three-dimensional sense," Heinrichs says. "It's fun and interesting to get an interplay going between very graphic and very sculptural elements, things that aren't normally thought of as being the same. Here we have a very sculptural environment, Lake Powell, and a very graphic environment in Hawaii. The final environment, out near Ridgecrest, is both very graphic and flat and sculptural at the same time."

ABOVE: At work on the Lake Powell set. BELOW: Tim Burton, center, preparing a shot on the lava fields of Hawaii. RIGHT: An action sequence at the Trona Pinnacles.

Building A City of apes

HEINRICHS, along with his core design crew of art directors, set decorators, and illustrators, began the process of designing the ape civilization. They took inspiration from a variety of sources including the primordial landscape of Hawaii's lava fields. Heinrichs wanted to bring a sense of history to the settings: "With the ape architecture we wanted the sense of an ancient civilization. Something about their culture seemed to call for resonance with early cultures in our own world—those that were the superior civilization of their place and time: the Egyptians, the Etruscans, the Mayans and Aztecs, a melange of different things we liked the look of."

The biggest set designed by Heinrichs was the city where the apes dwell, referred to in the original script as Derkein. Every square inch of a Sony soundstage was filled with a thoroughly imagined habitat to support the working life of an exceptional society of apes. Here they sleep, dine, raise families, play politics, wheel and deal their economy, entertain, gossip, and play out the intrigues of a lively citizenry. From their dwellings to their tablewear and coinage, every piece was designed by an art department charged with exploratory research and creative zeal.

Conceived as occupying a hillside within a lava environment, Ape City was a fantastical jungle enclave littered with towering rock statues, trailing vines, twisted undergrowth, and huge overhanging trees. Dominated by a central piazza and a rough road that cut through the entire set, Ape City featured a fortress at one end with numerous ape homes carved into the rock face all around. On one side of the set, the timbered balcony of Ari's home overlooks the main street, while on the other side a terraced dining area (also part of Ari's domicile) awaits guests. Doorways and windows are bathed in the flickering shadows cast by lighted torches; winding pathways

ABOVE: Mauro Borrelli's concept illustrations for Ape City. BACKGROUND: Ape City under construction at the Sony Studios. RIGHT INSET: Ari's balcony overlooking Ape City at dusk.

lead up to several different levels, including the quadrangle and wooden pens of the slave market run by the orangutan Limbo, where humans are processed when first brought into the city. "I think Ape City is the pinnacle of design," says Ralph Winter. "So many little nooks and crannies. So many beautiful textures and lines. The whole design is stunning. You'll really believe you're in another place when you're in Ape City."

Following a quarter-inch scale model, Ape City took four months to build on Stage 30 at Sony Pictures in Culver City. "At our busiest we had about a hundred people on stage," recalls Heinrichs, "plasterers, painters, sculptors, laborers, going towards this deadline and trying to work around each other. Part of making a set is the dance between all the different departments: first the wood goes up, then the foam or plaster or both, and then the painters come on, then the greens [non-sexist form of greensmen, the industry name for employees who arrange all plant materials on a set]. A time lapse film over the four months would have shown a whirlwind of activity attacking what seemed like an impossible deadline." Measuring 50 feet high by 130 feet wide, by 240 feet long, the set also made use of the stage's 10-foot-deep tank to give it added height. "That was part of the concept of the apes, that they live more vertically," says Heinrichs, "While all the many layers may be grounded, it almost feels like a giant treehouse. That just felt appropriate to the simian nature."

An incredible spectacle, Ape City drew many visitors during the four weeks the production filmed there. It also proved useful for helping the actors get into character. "I love Ape City," says Helena Bonham Carter. "It's like being in Las Vegas because you have no sense of time or day; it's a complete fantasy. You have the strong sense of being in a strange place."

LEFT: Concept drawing of Ape City by James Oxford. RIGHT: The central piazza of Ape City.

odyssey of a spaceship

ANOTHER key set was the space station, the USAF *Oberon*, where Captain Leo Davidson is stationed as the film begins. It's here that we first meet Davidson and the rest of the ship's crew, as well as the apes, mainly chimps, that are being used as test pilots. Heinrichs felt that the *Oberon* should be predominantly white, a clinical, calming environment to contrast with the lush tropical ambience of Ape City. "The idea was to go for very clean lines, creating a sense of calm and an almost sterile view of human existence in outer space," explains Heinrichs, who extended the apparent size of the set with cunningly positioned mirrors.

When Leo disobeys orders and launches himself into space to find his pet chimp, Pericles, who has gone missing, his pod gets caught in some kind of space storm and crashes to the surface of the ape planet, into a jungle bog. For the crash-landing scene as well as Leo's subsequent pursuit by apes through the jungle, Heinrichs built a jungle set, complete with water-filled bog, on stage at the LA Center Studios, after first exploring and ruling out real jungle locations. He decided to go with a stagebound set for reasons of practicality and design. "It became obvious that what we needed was the sense of a jungle, not a literal jungle." Plus, he says, there was the practical issue of stunts to consider. "There were a lot of

ABOVE: Concept drawing of Leo in the Pod.
RIGHT: Anne Ramsay as Chief Medical officer
Lt. Col. Grace Alexander overlooks Leo and
Pericles on the *Oberon*. RIGHT INSET:
Concept drawing by James Oxford of the
Oberon's animal cages.

flying apes, running apes, and a chase. If you build it, you can knock it down and push it out of the way. It became clear that real jungles didn't have anything on what we could do on stage." Heinrichs used large banyan trees, very sculptural root systems, and dense green canopies to produce a highly stylized environment "that supports the action but also says weird, scary, foreboding jungle."

The final set, built in the Trona Pinnacles, was a huge cathedral-like construction—nearly 300 feet high including the hill it stood on—in and around which the climactic battle takes place. This is a forbidden place to the apes, who call it Calima, later revealed to be the wreckage of Leo's ship,

ABOVE: Construction of the *Oberon* set. RIGHT: Matt Codd's concept drawing of the Calima ruins. BELOW: Mauro Borrelli's illustration of Leo's first encounter with the humans in the bog.

the *Oberon*, which crashed thousands of years earlier. Built from steel and foam at a cost of $1 to $1.5 million and anchored with concrete, the set was an impressive piece of design and a remarkable feat of engineering. The foam was coated with a hardening agent to allow it to withstand the desert weather. Once it was built, however, Heinrichs let it sit in the desert for a month or so to let the natural elements—dust and wind and sand—burnish it and give it a more realistic look.

LEFT: Concept illustration of the *Oberon* in space by James Oxford. BACKGROUND: The massive Calima set at the Trona Pinnacles. RIGHT INSET: The pod returns to the *Oberon*.

APES AND HUMANS

"people tell me I'm **simian** in a lot of ways. I don't know if I should take it as a **compliment...**"

Actor Mark Wahlberg

WHEN it came to casting his *Planet of the Apes*, Tim Burton had only one stipulation. "We wanted to get people that were really good actors," the director explains, "actors who could come through the makeup. I've dealt with makeup before, and you need performers strong enough to burst through the makeup, so to speak." Not everyone had the same idea, as producer Richard Zanuck notes. "One school of thought said: Why spend a lot of money on actors since they're behind these masks? Just get people. But we wanted their personalities to come through those masks, so you could really feel each individual."

"We have a stunning cast," says executive producer Ralph Winter. "They're all professionals, some of them big stars with a great body of work behind them. Their credentials lend dramatic credibility to the kind of movie we're doing." Burton seconds this idea. "We wanted people who would bring gravity to their roles, especially the ape characters, because it's a way to see our own humanity from a different angle. And since *Planet of the Apes* is basically about reversals," he adds, "we see the human characters, like Daena, almost as animals that have to learn to be human. That's what's fun about this material—we get to turn people's ideas about human and animal behavior inside out."

ari
Helena Bonham Carter

To play the only ape who believes humans have worth beyond mere slavery, and whose "relationship" with astronaut Leo Davidson is at the core of *Planet of the Apes*, Tim Burton chose Helena Bonham Carter, the British star of *Room with a View*, *Wings of the Dove*, and *Fight Club*. "Tim phoned me up and said, 'Don't take this badly, but you are the first person I thought of to play this chimp,'" she remembers with a laugh. "I didn't take it wrongly at all. I said, 'Why did you think of me?' And he said, 'I had this hunch you like to change and look different.' Having been typecast for what I look like, it was so refreshing to have a director ask me to do something that clearly wasn't because of what I look like. I was really flattered."

"I like actors who do different things," muses Burton. "You see them taking risks and not caring how they look, which in this film is quite important. I felt Helena would bring a real strength and sensitivity to Ari."

Bonham Carter, whose performance in *Wings of the Dove* earned her a Best Actress Oscar nomination, says she saw *Planet of the Apes* as an adventure. "I didn't really say yes to *Planet of the Apes*, it was Tim Burton. I knew it was going to be arduous, with the makeup and the hours, but also that it was going to be utterly different and bizarre and humorous and absurd. I always have time for the absurd. It was something I couldn't really say no to."

Her character represents the kinder, gentler side of apekind. "Ari is a human rights activist and she's disgusted with the way humans are treated on the planet," the actress notes. "They're pretty much subjugated, treated as slaves and pets, but Ari believes that humans have souls and the potential for intelligence and can be sophisticated. These are very heretical ideas on the Planet of the Apes. I meet Leo, save his life, and recognize in him a similar rebellious spirit to my own. I want to change the state of affairs on the planet. With Leo I recognize I can."

Thade
Tim Roth

I n direct contrast to Ari's sympathetic view of mankind stands Thade, the villainous commanding general of the ape army, who believes humans are vermin and wants to wipe them out. "He's a scary monster," says the British-born Tim Roth of his character, who not only commands the ape army but carries the added burden of a secret that could bring down the rule of apekind. "He's an interesting villain," notes Richard Zanuck. "He's the only one who knows that humans really might be smarter than apes. They have to be kept down, they have to be persecuted and restrained. He knows more about the human mentality than the humans do."

Burton says that Roth's disposition made him a natural for the role of Thade. "When I met Tim, he seemed really right because he's got kind of an ape personality," Burton laughs. "He's definitely the villain of the piece. He represents the purity of ape culture on a certain level." Roth agrees. "I suppose you would call him a purist, in that he doesn't like the human traits that are invading apedom. He's a bit of a Nazi."

Best known for his roles in independent movies such as *Pulp Fiction*, *Reservoir Dogs*, and *Little Odessa*, Roth has played memorable villains in the past, scooping an Oscar nomination for Best Supporting Actor for his Highland turn in *Rob Roy*. Portraying Thade, he says, gave him the opportunity to engage in some physical acting, particularly during those moments when Thade gives in to his ape side and goes wild, swinging from chandeliers or climbing up walls. "The idea is that he can go from absolute stillness to completely random and crazy behavior," Roth explains, "and we wanted to find several moments where that was possible. When chimps do go crazy, they really go crazy."

LEFT: Early costume test for
Thade's armor. OPPOSITE: The
final armor used in the film.

Attar
Michael Clarke Duncan

Following his breakthrough role as an oil worker who, with Bruce Willis, helped save the world in the asteroid extravaganza *Armageddon*, Michael Clarke Duncan has proved himself an actor of considerable range in both comedy and drama. His powerful performance as a death row prisoner in the Stephen King adaptation *The Green Mile* earned him an Oscar nomination. In *Planet of the Apes* the six-foot-five actor again brings his imposing physical presence to bear as the massively intimidating gorilla Captain Attar, second in command to Thade in the ape army.

Despite his character's size and demeanor, Clarke Duncan feels that Attar is something of misunderstood ape and that he even manages to redeem himself by the end. "It comes to a place where Attar is torn between what a general should do and doing what is right, treating people fairly," says Clarke Duncan. "He doesn't really hate humans. He's just going along with it because that's what he's supposed to do. Attar is sort of a good guy. He puts on the facade of a mean, terrible person, but he's not. He has that authority thing going on."

Clarke Duncan considers himself a huge fan of the original series and was thrilled to be involved in this latest addition to the *Planet of the Apes* canon. "I'm going to be part of film history," he enthuses. "I can't wait for opening weekend. I want to see how fans react to it."

Limbo
Paul Giamatti

If there had been a prize for being the biggest *Planet of the Apes* fan in the cast, it surely would have gone to Paul Giamatti, who says he was obsessed with the film series as a child. "I think I was probably four or five when the last one came out. I reacted especially to the gorillas, for some reason, which I guess most kids did. I think it was similar to why kids get into dinosaurs: they're big, powerful. I remember seeing all the movies, the TV show, having the dolls—and I think I had a little Ape City. I used to draw the dolls. I was really obsessed." So much so, in fact, that when Giamatti heard through a friend in the makeup department that there was going to be a new *Apes* movie, he called his agent and told him to get him a part. "I said, I have to do this," Giamatti laughs. "I've been living my whole life for this, you know?"

A gifted comedic actor whose numerous film credits include *Private Parts*, *Big Momma's House*, *Man on the Moon*, *Saving Private Ryan*, and *The Truman Show*, Giamatti brought a quirky sense of humor to his role as the unscrupulous orangutan slave trader Limbo, whose allegiance changes constantly throughout the movie. "Paul is very funny," declares Richard Zanuck. "He always seems to have the last laugh in every scene. I would say he's the Peter Lorre comic relief of this group.

"He's sort of an opportunist," Giamatti says of Limbo. "He'll sell anything to make money and get by." But working with humans has its price. "He's despised both by humans and by apes because he handles humans, and it's disgusting and dirty. He's lowered himself by working with humans," he observes. "But he's not a bad guy, I don't think. I've played a lot of sleazy guys in the past, and I'm playing a sleazy guy in this—but I'm an orangutan."

Krull
cary-Hiroyuki Tagawa

As far back as the original *King Kong*, Hollywood's portrayal of gorillas hasn't been too complimentary. "We don't stop to think of them as sensitive," insists Cary-Hiroyuki Tagawa, whose character, Krull, is based on a silverback gorilla. "And certainly Hollywood was responsible for that. I went back and saw some old footage of when they first started capturing silverbacks, and they played up the whole King Kong idea that they were dangerous. That is the biggest misconception."

Although his character now works as a servant in Ari's household, Krull actually is a former soldier who has been disgraced and demoted to domestic duty. "He is very much a warrior," says the Tokyo-born actor, who starred in *The Last Emperor*, *Mortal Kombat*, and *Rising Sun*. "A spirit-based kind of guy. As the story goes on, his true nature as a warrior is able to come out." Especially when it comes to protecting Ari. "He does things for her that he would not do for anybody else," Tagawa notes. "He's her protector, her guardian. But he's conflicted—he doesn't like humans." A longtime martial arts practitioner, Tagawa says his training helped him in both the physical and mental aspects of playing a gorilla. "The most critical part is learning to feel like you're 600 pounds," laughs Tagawa, "which sounds absurd. For a human, to weigh 600 pounds means you're 300 pounds overweight. But for a silverback gorilla, you're powerful at that size. You can move with the grace of a quadruped animal and stop on a dime. Things that, from my martial arts training, from my childhood fantasies as a ninja, I was always doing anyway. So I had a certain comfort level coming into it."

sandar
David Warner

"I represent the liberal wing of Apeville," claims veteran English actor David Warner, who has starred in more than 100 films, including *The Omen*, *Titantic*, *Time Bandits*, and *The French Lieutenant's Woman*. "I play Helena Bonham Carter's father. She's the animal rights conservationist in reverse: she cares about the humans and wants to treat them more sympathetically than most of the apes do. So I'm there to represent the social side of the apes."

Although Warner says he has never seen the original *Apes* movies, he once donned a gorilla suit for a memorable scene in the 1966 film *Morgan: A Suitable Case for Treatment*, and he has plenty of experience in wearing makeup. "Having to go through the makeup wasn't a problem for me. I have done shows before where I have had long makeups. And it really all depends on who's leading the gang. Tim Burton is leading this gang, and while I'd never met him before I'd heard by reputation how wonderful and how, dare I say it, sweet he is. So I knew that wouldn't be a problem. And Rick Baker makes it as comfortable as possible for us to wear." In fact, Warner adds, "I've never had so much fun working on something as we have on this."

captain Leo Davidson

mark wahlberg

For his human hero, Tim Burton was seeking not only a strong actor but someone who could ground the film emotionally, to whom audiences could relate amid all the weirdness. He found that in Mark Wahlberg, the former rap star who turned to acting with much success. "Mark has a real gravity to him, and a strength and a clarity set against this *Planet of the Apes*," Burton explains. "You really need that kind of anchor." Producer Richard Zanuck concurs. "He brings a sense of reality. There's a certain innocence about him, but he can be tough. He's in great shape physically."

After smallish roles in *Renaissance Man* and *The Basketball Diaries*, Wahlberg made his mark playing an adult-movie star in Paul Thomas Anderson's *Boogie Nights*, following this with a string of leading roles in *The Yards*, *Three Kings*, and *The Perfect Storm*. "He's a fine, underplaying actor," says Kris Kristofferson, Wahlberg's co-star on this film, "and that's the kind of acting I like. I believe him every time I see him. I appreciate that more than a theatrical type of a performance. And he's big enough to hunt bears with his shoulders. He's a good man."

Choosing his roles based on a film's director, Wahlberg was particularly thrilled by the idea of working with Burton, one he'd long admired. "It's always been about working with a great filmmaker, somebody who's interesting, and getting a chance to do something different every time out. All the roles I've chosen have been because of the filmmaker first and the material second. It's an honor to work with someone like Tim. I'm fascinated by the process of making films and have aspirations to make my own some day. Having an opportunity to learn from the best is a good thing, so I'm trying to take advantage of that."

Wahlberg says that when he signed on for *Apes*, he actually didn't know what role he was going to play. "I didn't read the script before I agreed to play the part," he admits. "I met Tim for literally five minutes and said, I'll do anything you want, and left crossing my fingers, hoping that if he did want me I wouldn't have to wear a loincloth. That was the main thing I was worried about. And I didn't really want to play an ape, only because I hate the makeup chair. This makeup is fantastic and Rick Baker is a genius, but for me to sit still for more than five minutes anywhere is really difficult." While Wahlberg escaped being turned into an ape, acting with them initially had its problems. "There were times when I wondered, what am I doing?

I'm acting opposite somebody in a gorilla outfit. But then I'd remind myself that Tim knows exactly what he's doing."

Leo's presence on the planet threatens to undermine the intellectual superiority and authority of the apes. "I don't try to change their world," Wahlberg notes. "I just want to get out of it. Unfortunately I don't have a way out, so in order to survive I have to try to do something."

Daena
estella warren

A former synchronized swimmer and member of the Canadian Olympic team, Estella Warren was working as a model when she decided to give acting a try. She'd discovered a taste for it while shooting a perfume commercial in Paris. Moving from New York to Los Angeles in 1999, she was barely off the plane when she landed roles in three movies in less than two weeks. *Planet of the Apes* was her fourth.

Unlike Linda Harrison's Nova in the 1968 film, Warren's character, Daena, is a warrior woman who helps lead the rebel humans' fight against the rule of the apes. "Some of the humans are slaves, trained to work with the apes, but there are some who rebel and don't want to follow the constraints the apes have put on them. Daena is part of the rebellious crew—she has a lot of animosity toward the apes because they've repressed her people for so long." Because the humans on the planet have never been socialized, Daena is like a wild animal in some ways, but over the course of the film she becomes less animal-like and more human. "She represents, even as a human, a kind of Beauty and the Beast in reverse," Tim Burton notes.

"There is that childlike aspect of her, the innocence and the aggression," says Warren. Her sports background helped her secure the role, she believes, in spite of her relative inexperience as an actress. "It seemed really natural for me to play this character because of the degree of athleticism that's involved. We're constantly running, and on horses and swimming and fighting with the apes."

"Estella's terrific," enthuses Linda Harrison. "She's the same age I was when I played Nova, except Daena is more of a feminist, and I like that. Nova was very submissive. I'm glad they're portraying her more as aggressive, standing up for herself."

karubi
kris kristofferson

Kris Kristofferson brings a grizzled gravitas to his role as Karubi, Daena's father and a leader of the human rebellion. Like Mark Wahlberg, Kristofferson started out as a singer and musician and made an equally successful transition to acting with films such as *Pat Garrett and Billy the Kid*, *A Star Is Born*, *Convoy*, and *Heaven's Gate*. And, like Wahlberg, Kristofferson says that working with Tim Burton was a special honor. "He's a hero in my house because I have eight kids. We've watched all of his films many times," he confides. "They turned me on to him way back, with *Pee-Wee's Big Adventure*. It's his positive energy that makes things work here. Tim goes out of his way to make everybody feel comfortable. There are long hours. Sometimes it's cold enough to hang meat, but he's always got enthusiasm and a passion for what he's doing. And he's having so much fun working that it's contagious."

Not that Kristofferson didn't have admirers of his own. "He is fantastic," beams Estella Warren of her onscreen father. "When we were shooting, he gave me some signed CDs of his, and I swear to God, it was one of the highlights of working on this film. And he's such a cool man. He's very laid-back, very genuine. Really funny. This guy is sixty-four years old and is in amazing shape. He's just incredible to look at."

"Part of the appeal of this job is that it's like playing, being a kid. Making believe," Kristofferson laughs. "I feel like a dolphin that just gets to play all its life. And when you're doing it in a place where the costumes and the sets and the situations are believable, it's very easy to slip into that suspension of disbelief, to feel like you're creating something new. This is definitely the most different thing I've done."

Birn
Luke Eberl

"There are two types of humans on the planet—the domesticated humans who live with the apes and are their servants, and the wild, feral humans," says 15-year-old Luke Eberl, whose character, Birn, is among the latter. "I'm the one of the wild children who live in the woods. Birn is strong, and he has fire in his heart. He's always quick to make a decision. Because he's in constant fear of the apes, his instincts are really sharp. He loves his father but is not as close to his sister, Daena."

After Leo rescues Birn and his family from being killed by the apes, the boy becomes attached to Leo, too. "He's really impressed by him—tries to follow him everywhere he goes and figure out what he's doing," says Estella Warren. "It's a very sweet kind of dynamic between the two of them. You see how much Birn admires him. He also has to be taken care of a little because he's quite a bit younger." For example, during the climactic battle scene Birn rides out on a horse and almost starts the battle singlehandedly. "Then I have to go out and save him," says Mark Wahlberg. Appearing in just his third movie, Eberl says he's been fortunate to witness firsthand the magic of cinema. "It's incredible what movies can do to stretch your imagination, go beyond the boundaries and create something incredible. That's what Tim is doing with this. He's got such a creative mind."

Thade's Father
Charlton Heston

Movie icon Charlton Heston is a big part of the reason why the original *Planet of the Apes* made such an impact: his performance as astronaut Taylor carried such power and conviction that it actually scared Tim Burton. And when rumors arose that Heston would have a cameo role in Burton's new film, fans eagerly speculated about what it might be—human or ape? Now we know: Heston appears briefly but tellingly in a deathbed scene as Thade's father, who imparts shocking revelations about the history of apekind to his son.

It was producer Richard Zanuck who persuaded Heston to revisit the *Planet*. Zanuck, who already had it in mind for Heston to switch sides and play an ape, convinced the star to come in for a four-hour makeup test—after which Heston agreed to come on board for a single day of shooting. "I was pleased when Dick Zanuck asked (insisted, really) that I undertake a cameo role in his new version of *Planet of the Apes*," says Heston. "He'd prepared the first film, which not only had been a huge success but had given me one of my very best parts. I look forward to the new version of *Apes* and expect it will have the same stunning impact with audiences around the world as the first one did."

Heston has starred in more than 80 feature films and nearly as many theatrical productions. After he made a splash on Broadway in the late 1940s, Hollywood came calling, and his movie roles are the stuff of legend: in *The Greatest Show on Earth*, *Ben-Hur* (which won him an Academy Award), *The Ten Commandments*, and *The Agony and the Ecstasy*, to name a few. His most recent film appearances include Kennneth Branagh's *Hamlet*, Disney's *Hercules*, and Oliver Stone's *Any Given Sunday*. He also returns to the stage regularly, most recently touring in A. R. Gurney's *Love Letters* with his wife of many years, Lydia.

"It's a great bookend to the first movie to have him involved," Ralph Winter declares. "It's like an Easter egg for aficionados to find out who is he playing and how that resonates in the story. When Dick pitched it, everyone said this is brilliant, this is fun. It's a perfect spot in the movie for him, and I think the fans will appreciate it."

ABOVE: Tim Burton directs Charlton Heston as the dying father of Thade.

woman in cart
Linda Harrison

As Nova, the savage human beauty who couldn't speak in the original *Planet of the Apes*, Linda Harrison owns a place in cinematic history. "I had just landed in Hollywood, so everything was outrageous to me," recalls Harrison of how she came to be cast in the 1968 movie. "I was dating Richard Zanuck at the time, and early in our relationship he talked about this incredible story that they very much wanted to film. So I knew a lot of the background. Then later he said, I think you would be great in the part of Nova."

Even at the time, Harrison says, she knew it was something special. "It had never been done, apes having the upper hand. We knew that we were doing something unique." Harrison and Zanuck later married and had two children, Harrison and Dean. Although now divorced, they have remained friendly. Harrison returned as Nova in the first *Apes* sequel, *Beneath the Planet of the Apes*, but since then has made only a handful of movies, among them *Cocoon* and *Cocoon: The Return*, both produced by her ex-husband. Although she appears only fleetingly in Burton's *Planet of the Apes*, as one of the humans brought into Ape City in a cart along with Wahlberg's Leo, Harrison's presence gives the movie a sense of completion. "Dick called and said, we'd like you to come on board for just a small part, for nostalgia's sake. And I'm as happy as can be about that." Even if Harrison still doesn't get to speak. "No," she laughs. "I'm afraid to talk. I mean, if we talk, we get beat up by the apes. So it's more of a look."

makeup magician
Rick Baker

ONE of Hollywood's leading creature creators, multi-Oscar-winning makeup artist Rick Baker is also a lifelong lover of all things ape. "They're just amazing animals," he enthuses, "so majestic, and in many ways better than humans. They're vegetarians, they don't kill for sport, they stay with their families. I became fascinated with them on so many levels." Baker's fascination has led him to create the most memorable screen apes of the last three decades, including the 1976 remake of *King Kong* (in which he also played the title character) and Sydney, the gorilla from *The Incredible Shrinking Woman*, as well the spectacular work seen in *Greystoke: The Legend of Tarzan, Lord of the Apes* and *Gorillas in the Mist*, for which he created the most convincingly realistic apes ever seen on film.

More recently Baker created the 25-foot-tall gorilla in *Mighty Joe Young* through a combination of animatronics, makeup, and computer effects. In fact, so pleased was Baker with his work on *Mighty Joe Young* that he thought he was pretty much done with cinematic apes forever. "I didn't think I could do much better than Joe," says Baker. But he didn't count of the lure of *Planet of the Apes*.

When Tim Burton came calling, Baker was just finishing up months of intense simultaneous labor on *The Nutty Professor II: The Klumps* and *Dr. Seuss' How the Grinch Stole Christmas*. He was planning to shut up his Glendale, California–based makeup shop and take a year off. But when Burton asked to meet with

> "I'm a makeup geek and an ape geek, and this is the ultimate film for me to do."
> MAKEUP DESIGNER RICK BAKER

> "When I look at Rick Baker, I see Merlin the magician. I see the big pointed hat, and that long ponytail that looks kind of cool."
> ACTOR MICHAEL CLARKE DUNCAN

him about creating an entire planet of apes, it was an offer he couldn't refuse. "I took it based on the title and Tim," explains Baker, who has known Burton since the latter worked at Disney; Baker won his third Oscar transforming the actor Martin Landau into horror-movie icon Bela Lugosi for Burton's *Ed Wood*. "I'm a makeup geek and an ape geek," he laughs, "and this is the ultimate film for me to do."

The makeup for the original *Planet of the Apes* won its creator, John Chambers, a special Academy Award for his efforts and has served as a stimulus for countless young makeup artists ever since. "I felt a lot of pressure taking this job," admits Baker, "because *Planet of the Apes* probably inspired more people to become makeup artists than any other movie. The makeups were great for the time—but basically they had one sculpture for each type of ape, which they duplicated. They sculpted the same face for all the orangutans, the same face for all the chimps, and for all the gorillas. The differences really came from the actors' varied structures underneath. They didn't try to make them dramatically different as characters. I like making characters and bringing out those differences. I said to Tim, there's so much more you can do. I really felt I could improve upon the first film."

ABOVE: Makeup designer Rick Baker.
RIGHT: Original concept illustration of Gary Oldman as ape by Rick Baker.

Rick BAKER
6-16-00

keeping
it real

EVEN though Baker thought Tim Burton was an ideal choice for the material, he was initially concerned that the director might want to take a direction with the apes that would be uncongenial to him. "A lot of his characters have a very specific look," Baker explains. "Dark circles around the eyes, very pale, sticky-uppy hair. And I said, if you want these apes to be Tim Burton–ized apes, I don't think I want to do it. I'm only interested if they're pretty real. He said, no, I want them real."

Burton and Baker began by discussing the types of apes that would be featured in the film, with Baker angling for baboons and gibbons as well as the eventual array of chimpanzees, gorillas, and orangutans. It was a conversation, however, that would change the species of one of the main characters. Thade, the villain

RIGHT: Actor Clay Fontenot wearing his Number Two mask. Fontenot was also a sometime number-one-mask ape. BELOW LEFT: Giamatti in full makeup. BELOW RIGHT: Baker's "white gorilla" Thade, following the script's original description.

RickBaker
© '00

of the piece, originally was written as a white gorilla, but after Baker told Burton how he felt about chimpanzees, Thade became one. "Chimps are the insane ones," says Baker. "Even though they're big, gorillas are much more passive. Chimps are the ones that frighten me. I've been this close to 450-pound wild gorillas in Africa and didn't feel the least bit threatened. I would be terrified to be near wild chimps because they just flip out. They start rocking and screaming and wave their arms around. As the big battle scenes were developed for the script, I said it would be great to have a bunch of crazy chimp guys just going berserk."

Although Baker had previously created screen apes using a combination of animatronics and makeup, for *Planet of the Apes* he felt makeup was the way to go. "I've done animatronic gorillas for films that were intercut with a real animal, and people did not know," he says. "I knew that could be done, but I didn't feel it was *Planet of the Apes*. This had to be actor-driven."

As with the original, Burton wanted to keep the film performance-based, so Baker devised makeups that gave the actors considerable freedom to move their faces. "You'll see a lot more subtlety," promises Burton. "We feel that's very important to this material and wanted to give the actors more opportunities of that kind." So while special effects technology and makeup materials have advanced greatly in the years since the first movie was made, Baker says his techniques and the materials used are pretty much the same as they were back then. "I used the same materials but applied them in a different way."

Because of the accelerated preproduction schedule, Baker and his crew had only four months to design and produce what would amount to hundreds of ape makeups before shooting began. Baker at first advised Burton and Zanuck that it could take up to a year to prepare for the film, but that wasn't in the cards. Fortunately, says Baker, "I'd just had the experience on *The Grinch* of doing ninety makeups a day for five months." Having had his crew's resources so thoroughly tested by that experience, he says, "I knew we could do this one."

LEFT: Baker's original Limbo design.
ABOVE: Actor Jo Jo Spangler in a
Number Two background mask.

Transformation

A Hank of Hair,
A Piece of Foam

TO transform Helena Bonham Carter, Tim Roth, Michael Clarke Duncan, and Paul Giamatti—basically the lead actors who appear in closeups—into apes was a painstaking process. First, Baker's team made life casts of each actor's head and teeth. Then, sculpting on these casts, Baker created each ape face individually. Once his designs were seen and approved by Burton, the makeups were then manufactured using foam latex prosthetics and special hairpieces tailored to the actor. "Every square inch of the appliance is carefully glued to the actor's face, so that when they move their face it translates through the rubber," describes Baker. Since the foam appliances couldn't be reused, new prosthetic pieces were required for every day an actor wore makeup.

By the time shooting began, Baker's crew, which at times numbered up to 100, was working around the clock to produce the necessary amount of ape makeup. The situation was not helped, Baker says, by delays in casting the actors who would play the leading apes. While Baker was at first determined to produce every ape makeup in a similar fashion, he decided, given the reduced time frame, that the only way to create the hundreds of apes the movie needed was to design three different levels of ape makeup.

The level that used individually sculpted prosthetics was referred to as "Number One." These took three to four hours to apply—longer for female apes, who had a beauty makeup applied on top of the ape makeup. That meant the ape actors had to arrive at 2:30 or 3:00 in the morning to begin their transformation, so they could be on the set on time, ready to begin shooting. "A lot depends on the performer," says Baker of the time involved in makeup. "If you sit there without moving or talking, don't take a lot of breaks and smoke cigarettes and drink coffee constantly, the makeup goes on very quickly. If you're taking breaks a lot, it can take a very long time. Tim Roth's makeup is very fast. Tim doesn't want to sit in the chair very long so he sits very still." Some of the actors used the time to learn their lines, others to sleep. "All you do is pop in a movie and let them do their thing," laughs Michael Clarke Duncan. "When I wake up, I'm no longer Michael Clarke Duncan, I'm Attar."

At the end of each working day, it would take up to an hour to remove the ape makeup, carefully so as not to damage the actor's skin. "Taking it off is actually worse than apply-

OPPOSITE: Helena Bonham Carter before and after the extensive makeup process. THIS PAGE: Actor Paul Giamatti being transformed into Limbo

ABOVE: A blend of yak hair (from tail and belly) and angora (for female chimp faces) was applied strand by strand. BELOW: Foam latex technician Bill Fesh pours the cake-batter-like mixture into injection guns, which, in turn, force the wet latex into the molds. RIGHT: Paul Giamatti's bust with Limbo neck piece, a gorilla face, and various finger molds used to create individual perfect-fit ape gloves. BELOW RIGHT: Makeup technician tying individual hairs into an ape glove.

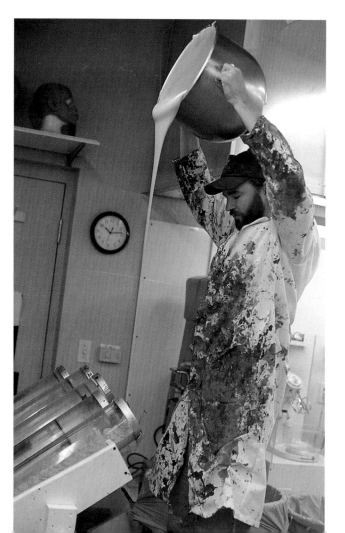

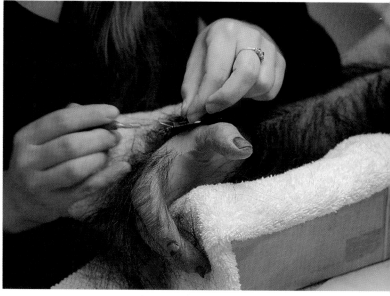

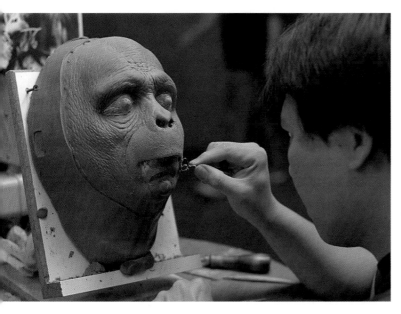

ing it," says Roth. "They have to take it off very gently, piece by piece, otherwise they'll tear your skin off. That's where I lose it sometimes. I become a wimp."

As well as facial prosthetics, each actor had to wear a customized set of fangs, "like a huge pair of dentures," says Baker, to extend their muzzle out as much as possible. "The teeth are the most difficult thing," says Paul Giamatti, who plays the oily orangutan Limbo. "They gave us practice teeth to learn how to speak, because it's hard to make sounds like P and V and F. And your lips are built out, it's not your own lips, which also makes talking very difficult."

"The funniest thing was all of us sitting around talking to each other with those teeth in, because you can't really speak properly," remembers David Warner, who plays Sandar, a chimp. "It's very hard not to crack up when people are trying to be serious or loving or angry, and all you hear is people going [mumble, mumble]."

The next level of ape makeup, referred to as "Number Two," was a very sophisticated over-the-head mask that fitted onto an actor's face. "They're made from the same material as the Number Ones, foam latex," Baker explains. "We sculpted them on life casts of the actors and made a vacuform plastic of their face, then glued this foam mask to the vacuform plas-

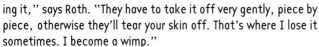

Ape makeup took between three and four hours to apply, which meant the ape actors had to arrive at 2:30 or 3:00 in the morning to begin their transformation.

tic. We'd paint dark around their eyes and strap this thing on their head. They can move the jaw around, though not the rest of their face."

Finally, there were the "Number Threes," which resembled slip-on Halloween masks, but of the highest quality. "It's a hollow rubber mask, but all the hairs are individually punched," says Baker. These were designed for use only in the background, but Baker refused to compromise on quality. "I wanted to make sure that when someone in a Number Three happened to be in the foreground, he would look good. So with the combination of these three different types, we were able to populate this film with a lot of interesting, different-looking apes."

ABOVE: Master sculptor Steve Wang creating Limbo. Wang was assigned exclusively to Limbo throughout the shoot. ABOVE RIGHT: Personality and talent were taken into account when matching makeup artist to actor. Here Bill Corso—Giamatti's exclusive makeup artist—works his magic at the Trona location. RIGHT: Helena Bonham Carter poses with her makeup team, makeup artist Toni G., left (who also headed the makeup department), and her assistant Deborah Patino.

Acting Through the Makeup

"RICK Baker is a genius," says Helena Bonham Carter, who plays the chimpanzee Ari. As one of the first ape actors cast, she became Baker's unofficial test chimp. "As soon as I met him, I had my cast done and thought, well, I'm in too far now," laughs Bonham Carter. The actress underwent ten weeks of elaborate tests. "How dark I should be. How much facial hair I should have. Whether I'd look too masculine because I have facial hair. Would I look too human or too apelike?

"It's interesting to think about what is attractive to us. Apparently some people find me bizarrely attractive as a chimp. But it's fascinating putting the makeup on. The first time it's a real shock. I had these thoughts, I look like a burn victim or somebody who's pre-aged. But I've gotten used to it." In fact, Ari was designed to be more attractive than your average ape.

"Her ears are not too big, and everything's softened," Baker says of Ari's look. "Chimps are really wrinkly, not attractive to us, so she has subtle wrinkles, a smoother complexion, a moderate amount of facial hair. Earlier I humanized her more, but it just looked ugly in a way. Too human would look like a freak and not an ape; more apelike is somehow less freakish. Helena's attractive to begin with. We gave her eyebrows—chimps don't have eyebrows. She wanted to be more purist about it, but the important thing is, does she look attractive? It was important to Tim that she be sexually attractive." Baker admits, however, that it didn't work on him. "I'm an ape-crazy guy, but I never wanted to make love to one."

Baker wasn't the only one with such concerns. "I was really worried about the relationship between my character and hers," Mark Wahlberg says, "because it anchors the story and without that it wouldn't have worked. For me to be attracted and fascinated by somebody in a chimp outfit was really difficult. But she's amazing in the part. She's so realistic and apelike, yet at the same time has this wonderful quality about her. She's pretty—that's what gets

"Rick came up to me very early on and said, you've got to move your mouth more. It looks dead."

ACTOR HELENA BONHAM CARTER

Leo's interest in the beginning. But she's also incredibly intelligent and caring, the kind of woman I would hope to meet on this planet. It's so bizarre—classic Tim Burton."

For all the actors who had to endure makeup, the experience was slightly unsettling at first. Not only contending with the long hours but also having to learn how to act with the makeup on. "It's tricky because you don't know what your face is doing," recalls Paul Giamatti. "You have to make the mask move, make it come alive," says Bonham Carter. "Because you can't actually feel anything. It's like having Novocain."

Baker, who appears in a cameo as a chimp smoking a hookah pipe, insisted that the actors really move their faces to make their expressions "read" through the makeup. "In the beginning I was running to Tim all the time saying, 'They're not exaggerating enough.' Actors are afraid to overact, even with lot of rubber on their faces. You can't be that way when you're wearing an appliance; you have to exaggerate. I made myself up one day and did a test. I'm not afraid to make a fool of myself—I've grown up gluing rubber on my face, so I've acquired the ability to move it quite well, and I've played gorillas in other films. When the actors saw it, Helena said, 'You're doing some great stuff. Can I steal some of that?' Please! I should have put makeup on earlier and run around and made faces, because it helped them to see somebody else moving it around."

"When you're behind that makeup, you can just let go," notes Michael Clarke Duncan, "because it's not you. Behind that makeup you can go crazy. You can go off the Richter scale."

"It's liberating," adds Bonham Carter. "You leave behind all your complexes about your own face—you've got this whole new one. Rick came up to me very early on and said, 'You've got to move your mouth more. It looks dead.' As an actor, when I'm not in makeup, one's taught all the time that less is more, so one doesn't move that much. If I do that under a mask, nothing happens."

Encountering the actors in ape makeup was a strange experience for their friends and family who happened to be visiting the set. "When you wear that stuff, people definitely treat you differently," insists Paul Giamatti. "When my wife came, she was really a little freaked out by it. And I forget I have it on. The weird thing is, it makes me a lot more aggressive. I'm not a very aggressive guy, but I definitely feel the mask loosens me up."

Once their makeup was applied, the actors had to spend the next ten hours looking after it. While Baker and his crew were on the set to help out, the job of protecting the makeup was the actor's, especially when it came to eating. "They issued mirrors for lunch," says Helena Bonham Carter, "because we didn't know where our mouths were and we had to protect the makeup. And frankly, you want to minimize how many people touch you up."

During meal times, actors playing apes would eat separately from those playing humans. "It's purely because eating is a depressing thing to do when you're in one of those makeups," says Tim Roth, "It's quite messy. You really don't want to be seen. You have to get used to where your mouth is: if you're aiming for your mouth as you normally would, you're going to hit latex. And because the lip is extended, food gets up in between

and it's disgusting. So eating becomes the most depressing time of the day. Also, you see others wandering around eating hot dogs or having a bowl of chili during the day, and you can't do that."

But despite the early call times and long hours in makeup, the actors remained largely positive. "I haven't heard one person complain about the makeup," insists David Warner. "I haven't heard one person talk about how uncomfortable it is. I haven't heard any moans at all. That's a rare thing, isn't it?"

Complaints may have been few, but if you spent any time on the set, you would have heard some strange noises. Ape noises, that is. "Tim Roth and Paul Giamatti are the weirdest ones on the set," laughs Michael Clarke Duncan. "They make these noises. Awk, awk. They sound like apes for real. It's as if they have embodied their characters. Their mannerisms are just like apes, and even when we cut they keep talking like apes."

ABOVE: Left to right, actors Jo Jo Spangler, Rick Baker, Chet Zar, and John Alexander in a scene from the central piazza. CENTER: Paul Giamatti aping for the camera.

Let's Go Ape

IN the original *Planet of the Apes*, the actors' efforts to move like apes were limited to shuffling around with their shoulders arched and their backs slightly hunched. For this version, Burton insisted his apes be as animal-like as possible. He wanted them to move realistically, be it walking, swinging from trees, or hurtling around a room. To this end the production set up an Ape School, lasting ten to twelve weeks, for all the principal actors. Numerous extras and stunt people also came to learn how to "go ape." "We're meant to be, as Tim says, 80 percent human and 20 percent ape," reveals Helena Bonham Carter. "We are anthropomorphized, so we're not pure apes. We're an evolved species."

"If we played them too much like real apes, then it would become like a bizarre *National Geographic* film," says Tim Roth, "which Tim wasn't particularly interested in doing. And if our apes behaved purely as humans do, again it wouldn't be very interesting. So it was a matter of finding a balance between the two."

In charge of the behavioral side of the actors' training was John Alexander, an ape specialist who had worked with Rick Baker on *Greystoke, Gorillas in the Mist,* and *Mighty Joe Young,* and

> "If we played them too much like real apes, then it would become like a bizarre *National Geographic* film."
>
> ACTOR TIM ROTH

who had played apes in movies himself. Alexander also was responsible for training the real apes used in the film, and even brought in several chimps for Burton and his cast to interact with during the rehearsal period. "John became a kind of behavioral dictionary for us," says Roth.

Mark Wahlberg, whose character had the most interaction with real apes, found that acting with chimps could be a scary proposition. "If you're on their bad side, you're in trouble," he observes. "They are so strong. And they play rough. When we were in rehearsals, Helena and I spent a lot of time with the chimps because the crew wanted us to be comfortable with them and them with us. I went to give Helena a hug once and they just attacked me—they're so protective. Both of them jumped on me and started pounding on me. It was pretty scary." Eventually the chimps learned that Wahlberg was the keeper of treats, and they got along fine.

Tim Roth's policy toward the chimps was total avoidance. "I don't particularly want to form any relationship with them. While they're very sensitive animals, they're still animals. They are incredibly strong. They are meat-eaters, and at times they're cannibals. They can be aggressive, and because they're so powerful they can act on that aggression. You have to be very careful. When we had real chimpanzees on the set, I stayed away from them."

LEFT: Limbo, hanging by his knees, takes a flower bath. ABOVE: Pericles and his trainers rehearse. RIGHT: Mark Wahlberg on the *Oberon* set with Pericles and Anne Ramsay.

finding the inner ape

HELPING the actors move like apes were stunt coordinator Charlie Croughwell and Terry Notary, a former gymnast and member of the famed Cirque du Soleil troupe, who now runs his own production company developing characters for circus shows. "The movement is going to make or break this film," asserts Notary, who previously worked with Croughwell on *The Grinch*. "I mean, the makeup is incredible. The actors are tops. The director is amazing. You have all the ingredients. But if you throw the actors in a suit and they can't move or look the part, then it's back to the old *Planet of the Apes*. This is the new generation. We needed to create something special here."

"I looked at the original *Planet of the Apes*," says stunt coordinator Charlie Croughwell, who hired Notary as a stunt performer and one of three movement coaches (the others were Sonny Tipton and John Alexander.) "I analyzed the way the people moved in monkey suits. Did they tell the audience they were monkeys, or did they tell us they were people in monkey suits? That's probably been my greatest concern throughout this picture: that the characters don't look like people, that they move like apes. We studied gorilla movement and chimp movement. Their attitudes in different situations, their aggressive behavior, their compassion."

Notary, who describes his job as "teaching the actors how to tap into their own ape," visited the zoo again and again to watch how primates moved. "Basically the primate is a very liquid animal; he spirals into a chair. You notice how subtle their movements are. Apes are so grounded and so direct. Everything they do is with a direct intention. There's no human quirks or thoughts to confuse the issue. When they want something, they go for it.

"We needed to loosen up the actors to approximate real ape body language. In essence we had to teach them

ABOVE: Terry Notary instructs Lisa Marie's Nova in the fine art of dining like an ape.

how to find their own sense of being primal and translate that into a character, because each person has their own way of moving and feeling. It's really about letting go. Losing all your inhibitions, losing all those little distracting thoughts and tapping into your animal instincts." It wasn't that simple, however. As Croughwell points out, "The way an ape moves is entirely different from how a human moves, because their bodies are built differently. We have short arms and long legs. They have short legs and long arms. They don't have the stride that a human does."

While the movement coaches worked with actors chosen by Burton for their skill as performers, Croughwell had to find stuntmen who could play apes. "We did our best to find short-legged, long-armed humans, but it was tough. With guys that weren't built like that, we had to teach them to compact themselves, bring themselves down into a more apelike stance. Aside from needing to be compact, you had to be able to leap better than most humans can. Primates have a great deal of power in their legs. I had to find stunt guys that were really strong gymnasts, who had the power to do what we needed. Then we assisted them with cables."

Working first with stuntmen, Croughwell, Notary, Tipton, and Alexander came up with a variety of concepts for how the apes could move. They videotaped these and presented them to Burton, then incorporated the director's adjustments. "When we started out, they were all walking like humans. So we had them roll their feet so they're walking on the outsides, almost bowlegged. Cowboys make great apes because they're bowlegged. It's difficult to teach a person with long straight legs to be an ape, because they have to bend their knees out and it's very painful. It's a long process: We worked our way from standing upright, getting your shoulders and chin in the right posi-

> "We started calling it Simian Academy, just because it sounds a little classier than Ape School."
> ACTOR PAUL GIAMATTI

tion, the butt out, all the way down to the legs and feet. For chimps, you get your butt forward. For gorillas, you get your chest out. Orangutans are really gangly."

Once Burton had approved the various ape movements, the videotapes were shown to the actors, who developed their own characters based on what they saw the stuntmen do. "We had to find little things that worked for each actor individually," says Notary, who spent time on set critiquing the actors' movement during filming as well as doubling for Tim Roth. "One person imagines he's walking on ice in a rink. Another thinks of walking on railroad tracks, and another person feels like he's got a beach ball between his legs. Everybody has their own thing that makes it work."

Bonham Carter attended ape school three to four days a week for five weeks. "It was taken very seriously," she notes. "At first I failed. I have absolutely no concentration, which I thought might be very chimplike. But no. You have to be 'in the zone.' You'd have to constantly tell yourself you're a quadruped. It's a bit like dancing. The image that really worked for me was to imagine wearing a diaper full of stuff that I didn't want to spill. You had to really be in your body. Apes have an economy of movement, so you have to be immensely focused. When we humans sit down, we rearrange ourselves and fidget; apes will just sit. And if they get bored they'll do something else. But their focus is absolutely 100 percent, which was very useful for me to learn.

"I thought everyone should go through ape school and have to discover their inner ape. They're much more sensual and tactile than we are. They've got a much better

ABOVE: Terry Notary instructs ape extras on the Trona set.
RIGHT: Jo Jo Spangler plays a stringed instrument with hands and feet on the Ape City set.

sense of smell. Their intuition is much greater. So it was a very fertile period for me, even though I got an F at first." The actress laughs, "But Paul Giamatti sailed through it. He was always brilliant."

"They taught us how to walk like apes, pick up weapons, jump, come down stairs, anything you can think of—like an ape," offers Michael Clarke Duncan. "They were on the set too, critiquing you after every take, tell you how you were doing in your ape character. 'For that walk, you have to move like this.' Everyone had a specific walk. Since I'm a silverback gorilla my walk is different from Tim Roth's character, who's a chimpanzee. His is more bowlegged. Mine is with slightly bent knees, but an upright back and rounded shoulders."

As the ferocious Thade, Roth positively reveled in turning the clichéd view of cuddly chimps on its head. "He would become quite sharklike and focused and quiet. The idea was that he would suddenly be in your face, looking at you. There can be something quite terrifying about the way a chimpanzee will look at you, because you don't know what it's going to do. We wanted Thade to be somebody who, if he walked into a room you never quite knew what to expect from him. And we just played around with the violence as much as we could."

"Anything Thade does, he does it big," says stunt coordinator Charlie Croughwell. "He's a very physical chimp, so he doesn't just go get on a horse. At first we didn't want the apes to ride horses at all, but once that was settled we tried to take it a step further and say, how would a chimp actually mount a horse? Would he go up and grab the saddle horn, or grab the reins and put his foot in the stirrup and swing his leg up? Probably not. He would run up a wall and then leap across to the horse and land on its back."

As actors have done in countless more conventional movies, many of them also got horseback-riding lessons. "They'd ride for two or three hours every day, whenever they were available," says Croughwell, "just to get comfortable with riding. A lot of them had never ridden or had not since they were children, and you have to get to a point where you're comfortable, where you understand what the horse is going to do. A horse has a mind of its own, and when it decides to do something there's nothing you can do about it unless you're experienced. The more experience they have, the safer they'll be and the more they can do, which means I don't have to use stunt doubles for everything. I can get more stuff for Tim."

OPPOSITE: Tim Roth as Thade mounts his horse chimp-style. ABOVE: Ari exhibits apelike behavior. LEFT: Guy Hendrix Dyas's concept drawing of Thade on an armored horse.

THE SHOOT

"I call Tim Burton a **mad scientist,** because he looks really weird. You know how Albert **Einstein** looked all crazy? That's the way Tim Burton is."

Actor Michael Clarke Duncan

THE re-imagined *Planet of the Apes* began filming on November 6, 2000, on the shores of Lake Powell, a manmade lake in the Arizona desert. Among the first few scenes to be shot was a raid on an ape encampment by a band of humans and apes led by Mark Wahlberg's Leo, Helena Bonham Carter's Ari, and Estella Warren's Daena, and their subsequent escape on horseback across a river. "One of the movie's key elements is that water is a barrier to the apes," Winter explains. "Apes don't swim. Leo discovers this and uses it to outsmart them. In this scene he steals their horses and drives them across the water. We had to find a safe place to stage that. The lake's 800 feet deep in spots and very cold, so we're taking every precaution for the horses and the humans." Further complicating matters, the water level on the lake had dropped since the location was initially scouted, forcing the production to pump in a quarter-million gallons of water before filming could commence.

"We swam our group of heroes—some actors and some stunt doubles—across a part of Lake Powell that was not much above freezing point," reveals stunt coordinator Charlie Croughwell. They had to heat the water from around 40 degrees to an acceptable 68 degrees with an enormous propane device to enable the actors and horses to bear it. "The human characters don't wear much so it was very difficult, and very tough on the horses. On one extreme the humans who aren't wearing much are freezing to death, and on the other extreme, the doubles in ape costumes would take on water and end up weighing about 500 pounds—which was obviously dangerous while trying to hang onto a horse." As the good guys escape, the apes pelt them with flaming fireballs. "That presented other dangers," Croughwell continues, "because the ape costumes are not flameproof, so you've got a lot of potentially flammable guys running around throwing fireballs."

By Land, Water, and Time Warp

FOR producer Richard Zanuck, revisiting the same location where the original *Planet of the Apes* was shot thirty-three years earlier was an emotional experience. "It's almost overwhelming to be here," he admits. "The whole thing is like a giant time warp. We shot the opening of that film here and about a mile away. It seems like another lifetime ago. It was another lifetime ago."

Filming at Lake Powell took place on a cove called Independence Bay, where the ape encampment was erected. To get there, cast and crew took a twenty-minute boat ride from the opposite shore, where they were staying. The only way

to ship people and equipment in was by water. "It was like staging an invasion of Lake Powell," muses Zanuck, "with horses, a lot of apes, practically all of our cast. The makeup crew alone for this location is enormous." Ralph Winter concurs. "We're spending hundreds of thousands of dollars on boats and barges and marine personnel. Everything comes on the water. If you want to use the bathroom, it's on a barge. The apes' tents were custom-made months ago in Los Angeles and had to be erected on the beach against the winds here. The seas were very rough and very cold. So it's been a little dicey from that standpoint. Some of our actors are wearing skimpy outfits, and it's tough on them. But it looks great."

For actors like Helena Bonham Carter, the workday began at 2:30 A.M. and lasted long into the night. "It's a long, long day for her, sitting in

LEFT: Drawing of the interior of the Calima ruins by Matt Codd.
ABOVE: Helena Bonham Carter and Tim Burton on the Ape City set between takes.

the makeup chair," says Zanuck. "She's able to sleep a little during the procedure, but I don't know how good that sleep is. It's very tough, but she looks fabulous." Bonham Carter says that the Lake Powell scenes brought home the full scale of the production in a way she hadn't really grasped before. "I remember thinking, my God, this is a huge undertaking. It's massive. When I got my first call sheet and saw the number of people involved in making this film, it was kind of awe-inspiring."

Although Tim Burton has a well-deserved reputation as a master of visual images, he is also renowned for his rapport with actors, who obviously adore working with him. "It's the first time I've actually looked forward to going to work," Mark Wahlberg enthuses, "even though I know I'm going to get beat up. It's because Tim is so funny and so willing to let everyone have their say and develop their characters along with him. I've gotten beaten up more in this movie than in all the other movies I've been in, but Tim's made it easy on everybody. He's very concerned with safety and would never put anyone in a really threatening situation. I don't have a problem doing whatever he wants me to. But if it's between Michael Clarke Duncan and myself, I try to suggest that maybe Tim use a double—the guy is really big and really strong."

"For someone who has such a specific vision, Tim is surprisingly collaborative and open and generous," Helena Bonham Carter offers. "He's intensely novel and sweet and so funny, which is great; it entertains one through the long days. He's full of motion. Hands are flailing. He's utterly unaware of himself physically, so he's always verging on killing himself. We all worry because he will nearly hurl himself off the set by mistake, because he isn't aware of quite where he puts his body." In fact, Burton broke a rib during filming. "I watched him trip over, fall down, bash his head, bruise his elbows and his knees on a daily basis," laughs Tim Roth. "You could almost put bets on which part of his anatomy he's going to damage on which

"It was like staging an invasion of Lake Powell, with horses, a lot of apes, practically all of our cast. The makeup crew alone for this location is enormous."

PRODUCER RICHARD D. ZANUCK

day. But as an actor's director," Roth turns serious, "he entrusts you with the character completely. It was a smart move to get actors to play the apes. He could've just had stunt guys do it. But to bring the characters to life, I think he was right. It takes somebody like him to recognize that."

"He is very mad professor-like," concludes Bonham Carter with affection. "He's eccentric, obviously, but all intuition and instinct and heart. Not the most articulate person—when he gives you a note, you'll realize he's probably said about three words to you and none of them relate to each other—but somehow it will make complete sense. He knows exactly what he wants."

"Tim is one of the funniest directors I've ever worked with," chimes in Paul Giamatti. "Obviously he brings that visual sense, but those guys aren't necessarily great directors to work with as an actor. Tim is. One of the main things is how much fun he's having, and how he communicates that to you. That's really important, especially when you have a monkey mask on. He even looks a bit like a monkey, and I think that helps. I'm serious, he looks a bit like a monkey."

After a week of main unit work at Lake Powell, the production moved into the less problematic environment of the LA Center Studios in downtown Los Angeles to shoot the forest interiors, where Leo's pod crashes to the planet and he is pursued by apes through the jungle. Here, too, were filmed the scenes inside the spaceship *Oberon*. Then the show moved on to the Sony lot at Culver City for four weeks of filming on the massive Ape City set. The climactic battle scenes were shot at the Trona Pinnacles set over three weeks, after which the production returned to LA Center, with a final trip to Hawaii for a few days' work in the lava fields.

ABOVE: Producer Richard D. Zanuck and Helena Bonham Carter as Ari on the Trona set.
OPPOSITE BACKGROUND: The jungle set during construction.
OPPOSITE INSET: Leo in the pod.

LEFT and ABOVE: Exterior and interior drawings of the ape army tents by Guy Hendrix Dyas. BELOW: Custom-made tents erected on the beach at Independence Bay.

Battles on and off the screen

THE Trona Pinnacles proved to be an even tougher locale than Lake Powell for the *Planet* production. This vast, desolate stretch of California desert threw its worst at them: high winds, freezing conditions, and heavy rain made filming difficult, sometimes impossible. "Historically over the past decade they've had half an inch of rain every year. We got seven inches in the three weeks before we were due to arrive," explains Ralph Winter. "It was a mess." The production had built a seven-mile-long road leading from the highway to its base camp at Trona, but the rain and mud prevented even trucks from driving in, forcing Winter to import 75,000 cubic feet of gravel to make the road passable.

Then there was base camp itself. "The biggest I've ever seen in my life," marvels Winter. "We have 100 vehicles, 40 drivers, four honey wagons [trucks that transport out waste from the ranks of porta-potties brought in]. The size of the operation is astonishing, but that's what it took to put these apes on camera every day. And that's really where the expense is. It's the hours of makeup and wardrobe, cleaning it and setting it up. It's a 24-hour operation, keeping all these people going—like a little city." And running such a city required military-style precision to have cast and crew, which often totaled a thousand, ready each day to film the great battle scene between the humans, led by Wahlberg's Leo, and the apes, headed by Tim Roth's Thade.

The actors playing the lead apes—Roth, Helena Bonham Carter, Michael Clarke Duncan among them—would arrive on set between one and two in the morning to begin the makeup process, so that Burton could begin to roll by eight o'clock. Background extras, arriving between three and four, were passed through an assembly line to be made up as either apes or humans. "The background apes come in pretty early to get the baseball black around their eyes, around their nose and mouths so the ape head looks seamless," says Winter. "Then they go through 45 minutes to an hour of wardrobe. They may have a tune-up with the two military commanders we've brought in for Ape School. We might have them march around

for a while, do some of the ape movements to be sure they get that right—the timing, the formations. And then bus them down to the set. Background humans go through something similar. Their wardrobe is just as complicated: they have body makeup to make them look dirty, like they've been living out here for years. There are all these people to get ready every day."

Working in parallel to Rick Baker's makeup crew was the wardrobe crew guided by costume designer Colleen Atwood, who has costumed such films as *The Mexican*, *Silence of the Lambs*, *Philadelphia*, and *Little Women*, which earned her an Oscar nomination. She had worked with Tim Burton on *Sleepy Hollow*, as well as *Edward Scissorhands* and *Mars Attacks!*, and they quickly got on the same wavelength about what these costumes should be. As with Baker's job,

OPPOSITE: The production's Trona basecamp included more than 100 vehicles, which supported a cast and crew of up to 1,000. ABOVE: An extra enjoys a hot meal between takes. CENTER: The costume assembly line.

"There are many, many
challenges to dressing
a chimpanzee."

COSTUME DESIGNER COLLEEN ATWOOD

her first huge challenge was the scarily minimal time available to design and manufacture well over a thousand costumes, including very different looks for the spaceship crew, the feral humans on the planet, and a multilayered society of apes. "Not to mention," says Atwood, "coming up with new concepts during shooting as the script would evolve. The whole time I was running the shoot, I was also continually designing and manufacturing costumes, up until the last day of filming. And there was nothing in this movie you could really shop for—it's all created."

Costuming this film was never about copying the original movie, Atwood says, "though we did throw in a little homage here and there—like the white suits on the *Oberon* crew. And it was useful to have the earlier film for reference." They did use some of the same materials: "tons and tons of leather, hair of course—ours is mostly yak hair on a knitted backing, so it stretches and fits around body parts. We have it made in different degrees of fineness and lots of colors." But Atwood also made extensive use of materials unknown to the 1968

ABOVE LEFT: Drawing of Pericles'
costume. ABOVE: Early concept
drawing of Attar's armor.
LEFT: Concept drawing for
a senator costume.

98

LEFT: Sculpture of Thade's breastplate used by mold makers to create the finished armor. ABOVE: Detail of the ape army costumes. RIGHT: Concept drawing for Thade's armor.

filmmakers: "We're using lots of a tech fabric made of PVC, which can resemble fake leather and many other textures and surfaces. I worked with a textile artist named Jane Clive to create a PVC-based stretch fabric for the humans, sort of a three-dimensional material almost like reptile skin, that would fit tightly on people's bodies. Then it's painted with layers of copper and blue and turquoise and greens: colors like you'd see on certain reptiles.

"We wanted the costumes to echo the environment at the Trona Pinnacles, so the pattern for silk-screening the paint was based on aerial views of parched land and animal skin, blown up and drawn onto a screen. In parts of the movie you don't see the colors because there's so much dust layered on top of it. These costumes also have to keep the actors comfortable, because though it's not supposed to look like it, it was cold out there."

At its peak of activity, Atwood's crew numbered around 100. Sculptors were the first stage in creating the warrior apes' armor, sculpting her designs on large forms. Mold-makers then translated the sculptures into fiberglass or other materials used for the armor. Cutter/fitters were kept constantly busy fabricating "soft" costumes, including body suits worn by the ape actors under their costumes. Seamstresses assembled all the costumes by hand, usually in multiples of each. Bootmakers and jewelers rounded out the costume cast. Then there was Atwood's shooting and maintenance crew, who arrived on the Trona set at 2:30 A.M. to start getting apes and humans suited up for the day. "It's very high maintenance all day long," sighs Atwood.

Most of the extras on the Trona set were local people employed to swell the ape and human armies. "When we first looked at locations it was 120 degrees, and we were really concerned because obviously the ape suits are very hot," recalls second unit director Andy Armstrong. "But when we went to shoot there, it was really cold, so the worry was not so much for the apes but for the humans, who were very scantily clad. All the local extras we found were fantastic. It was amazing how much people enjoyed being there. We even had some women, housewives, who came along to work as apes and didn't miss one day of the whole thing. They're marching over rough terrain, charging, working in dust, beating themselves up all day long."

Filming would last until sunset—in February this came between 4:30 and 5:00 in the afternoon. But work continued

after filming wrapped, right through the night. "They would take all the stuff off the extras, clean it, repair it," says Ralph Winter. "A repair crew comes in and finishes by nine, ten o'clock at night. Then it starts all over again." On some days, however, the conditions proved too disruptive. "There was just too much wind and rain coming at us, so we battened everything down and waited it out," says Winter. "It delayed us a couple of days, but we used that time to prep and try to stay on target."

For much of the three-week shoot at Trona, the main unit under Burton's direction filmed alongside the second unit led by Andy Armstrong, whose credits include *Charlie's Angels* and *Galaxy Quest* and who had previously worked with Burton on two action-packed commercials for Timex watches.

"Traditionally second units do stuff that's highly time-consuming or has long setups or is predominantly action," Armstrong notes. "Tim uses me in slightly different ways, because a lot of what we're doing on this picture is very experimental. There's a very fine line between what looks really scary or interesting with the apes, and what looks terrible and hokey. So often we'll experiment together to find what works, or he'll set the flavor of the scene and I'll sweep along afterward."

Just as Burton was adamant that his apes would move like real apes, he was determined that they would behave like wild animals during fight scenes, lending the action a ferocity and impact never approached in the original movie. "You'll see great action in this picture," promises Richard Zanuck, "apes flying right at you and wonderful battle sequences: ape against ape, ape against man. Apes swinging from trees, jumping out of bushes, traveling at great speed, passing horses, running. We're using every stunt in Tim Burton's bag of tricks—and it's a very big bag."

ABOVE: Detail of the fabric used for Daena's costume.
LEFT: An early rendering of Daena's costume. RIGHT: Extras on the Trona set, most of whom were local residents.

100

stunt masters

"**WHEN** Tim asked me to come on board, it was to really do something with apes that couldn't have been done at the time the original was shot," says second unit director Andy Armstrong. "To show the terrifying speed and power that a real primate has, which is somewhere between five and seven times the strength of a man—huge acceleration, great impulsive speed."

When Armstrong was choreographing the film's battle scenes, he had to make sure they all fit with Burton's unique visual style. "My job has been to deploy the action elements I'm used to working with, but mold them into something that fits with a Tim Burton picture. Hopefully there's a weirdness to the action that's not been seen before. We've all seen big battle scenes with horses, people, Indians, cowboys, armies—but we haven't seen a battle with characters that are not quite human yet not completely alien. They're very powerful, very fast; you see them overtaking galloping horses. It's really scary when there's lots of them screaming across the desert, and they can tear you apart."

Once Burton and Armstrong had outlined the various action sequences, it was up to stunt coordinator Charlie Croughwell to implement them. "We would ask, can they jump this distance, this height, and at this speed? Then Charlie would bring in his team to work out how we physically enabled someone to get from point A to point B, whether we could release them or knock them off a horse or whatever," says Armstrong. "We've done a lot with wire-assisted gags, decelerators, and ratchets, so the apes can jump and land on a precise spot. Charlie and all the stunt guys have done a fantastic job of making the physical movement different from anything seen before. You may have caught glimpses in a zoo, but you certainly haven't seen it with a creature that interacts and talks with humans yet can leap around and fly through the air and do somersaults. It's a careful blend of mechanical assistance and real gymnasts who can do some weird things."

The production set up a special, three-day ape school out in the desert to train the 200 or so extras drafted to play apes during the battle scenes. In addition to getting a crash course in ape movement, they were put through their military paces by several marines shipped in for that purpose. Throughout, Armstrong was aware that just one ape who looked like a man in a monkey suit would ruin the illusion. "Some people could be fantastic athletes, but they couldn't do the motion convincingly. And physically it's very tough on both the stuntmen and the extras. If they get too tired, they stop looking like an ape. You can have 200 people in the frame, but if there's a couple at the back looking exhausted, your eye goes straight to them and ruins the whole thing. So it's about watching every person in there."

During the battle, the apes drop down from two legs onto all four and speed across the desert. This particular quadruped movement the filmmakers termed "loping." "It's

LEFT: Preparing stunt performers for wire work.
ABOVE: Behind the scenes as Estella Warren fends off attacking chimps.

much like what chimpanzees and monkeys do in the wild, but we're taking it a step further," says Ralph Winter. "These apes have perfected loping to increase their speed tremendously. They can outrun a horse." Croughwell came up with the idea while watching videos of gorillas running. "Terry [Notary] was out at my house and we were trying to figure out how these guys would charge into battle. When they get mad, they have to charge, and it has to be real high energy. So we were trying to develop some system to sell the power and speed of an ape—because they can travel much faster than a human can—yet make it look believable."

As Notary ran around on all fours in his garden, Croughwell watched him and thought, "God, it's just not fast enough. It's looks a little too human." Then he had a brainwave, remembering another film in which he'd made Robin Williams appear to run across the countryside at 30 mph (*What Dreams May Come*, 1998). "What we did with Robin was use a traveling conveyor belt, which I still had. So we rolled out the conveyor belt, hooked it up to the back of my truck, put Terry on it, and towed

it around my property, shooting video. Then we towed Terry, on the conveyor belt, past some horses, and it looked like he was outrunning them. When we showed it to Tim and Philippe Rousselot later, Philippe said, 'I've seen this five times now, and I cannot figure out how you did it. What's the trick?' Everyone loved it. You can't see the conveyor belt, you have no idea it's there, and it looks like they're actually traveling that fast."

Still, finding people to lope was far from simple. "Although it looks easy when you see a real ape doing it, they're much more powerful than we are and have much shorter legs. So it's much harder for our guys to do it," says Armstrong. They auditioned hundreds of people to find some who could lope for any sustained length of time, eventually finding about a dozen. These were pulled through the desert on a 100-yard-long mat while doing their lope. "We tow them at 25 miles an hour," explains Croughwell, "and they appear to be screaming across the desert. It's both difficult and quite dangerous, because they'd fall off. Imagine running on your hands and knees and

ture, and Chris Lebenzon's cutting has a very fast style. So it will be completely convincing that there's at least a hundred apes loping across the desert."

The apes' ferocious agility won't be entirely confined to the battlefield. As screenwriter Larry Konner points out, "Tim had to have at least one place in the movie where an ape would go what he called 'apeshit'." That character was Thade, who throws an impressive temper tantrum when he receives some bad news. "What would a chimp do if he had a temper tantrum?" Croughwell muses. "Well, they rip things apart, jump all around, leap from place to place. So we took it a little further than an actual chimp could. Thade scales a wall, climbs and swings out on vines, takes his sword out and hacks a chandelier down. Then he leaps out over the chandelier, lands on his horse, and rides away."

Performing the stunt was Tim Roth's double, Terry Notary. "Terry is on a wire the whole time," says Croughwell, "so he's really a puppet on a string. We actually bounced him from one place to another in one shot, and we had control over the amount of force when he hit the horse. When we first rehearsed it, we brought Terry in really light, landing him about three inches above the horse's back so the horse would get a sense of what was going to happen. Then we gradually lowered him to a point where he was making full contact with the horse."

Unlike some actors, Roth feels no compulsion to do his own stunts and has nothing but praise for Notary's physical dexterity. "It takes two people to play a character like this," he notes. "When we did the huge leaps, using the ratchets and wires, I tried a couple but ended up saying, 'You do it.' I don't have the testosterone of an actor who needs to do all his own stunts and break legs. I'm really not interested in that.

falling over at 25 miles an hour." Armstrong agrees. "It's painful and exhausting." To assist the lopers, Croughwell used wires, like a bungee cord, to take some of the weight off, "to keep their bodies low to the ground and their butts down." Croughwell is especially proud of his achievement. "I think it really is a cool look. It may have been used once before but certainly never with as many elements as we had. We've combined it with galloping horses and dust machines and wind."

While Burton prefers not to rely heavily on computer-generated effects, some visual effects work was employed to give the impression of hordes of apes marching and loping across the desert. Industrial Light & Magic, the world's leader in VFX creation, lent its skills to several areas of the film, notably replicating the legions of apes that make up the ape army. "Eventually we're going to have at least a hundred apes galloping across the desert," says Armstrong. "But we're not relying entirely on that. We've done some other trick stuff. It's a mix-

ABOVE LEFT: The loping chimps attack. ABOVE: Stuntman Clay Fontenot rehearses with Luke Eberl, as Birn, on the Lake Powell set.

Terry was involved with me in the Ape School, so he knows exactly what I want from the character and can move in the way I want, so we blend nicely. When I'm doing my stuff he watches me to make sure it doesn't get too human on the movement level. And when he's doing stunt stuff I do the same for him. It's a great relationship to have."

Another stunt-intensive scene takes place in the jungle, when Mark Wahlberg's Davidson has crashed his pod into a bog, escapes from the water, and gets chased through the trees by apes. "He climbs on shore and then starts to hear rustling sounds in the jungle, and he doesn't know what's going on," describes Croughwell. "The next thing you know, humans are blasting through the jungle. He starts to run with them and gets really frantic. Suddenly you see dark figures flying through the trees."

Using a variety of wire rigs linked to decelerators and descenders and ratchets, Croughwell could make his stunt apes fly through the treetops, drop out of the branches, grab the humans, and take them back up into the trees. "The challenge with flying guys through the trees is designing the set around the fly rigs. You can't just build the set and then try to insert fly rigs into it because branches cross our cables, cross our wires, so the apes' travel would be restricted." To play one of those apes, Croughwell observes, takes great skill. They needed to be strong gymnasts, "not just on floor exercises but high-bar guys, because they understand the concept of grabbing hold of a bar, swinging up on it, and leaping off to another bar, or a tree limb, then just launching out of the tree. We then decelerate them to the ground. But they have to be able to hold a certain position. The chimp position, we call it."

LEFT: Stuntman Jayson Dumenigo, on the wire, rehearsing the jungle attack scene. RIGHT: Storyboard sequence by Michael Jackson of the jungle chase.

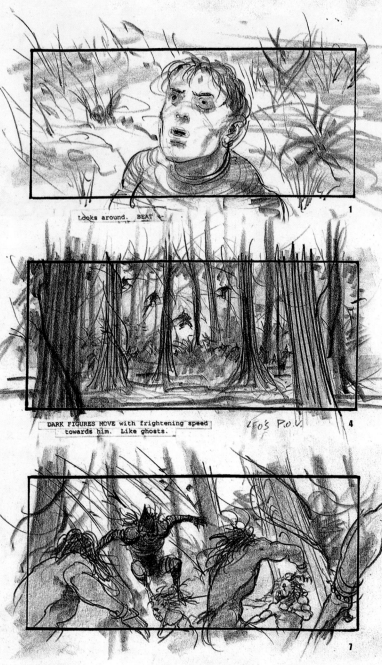

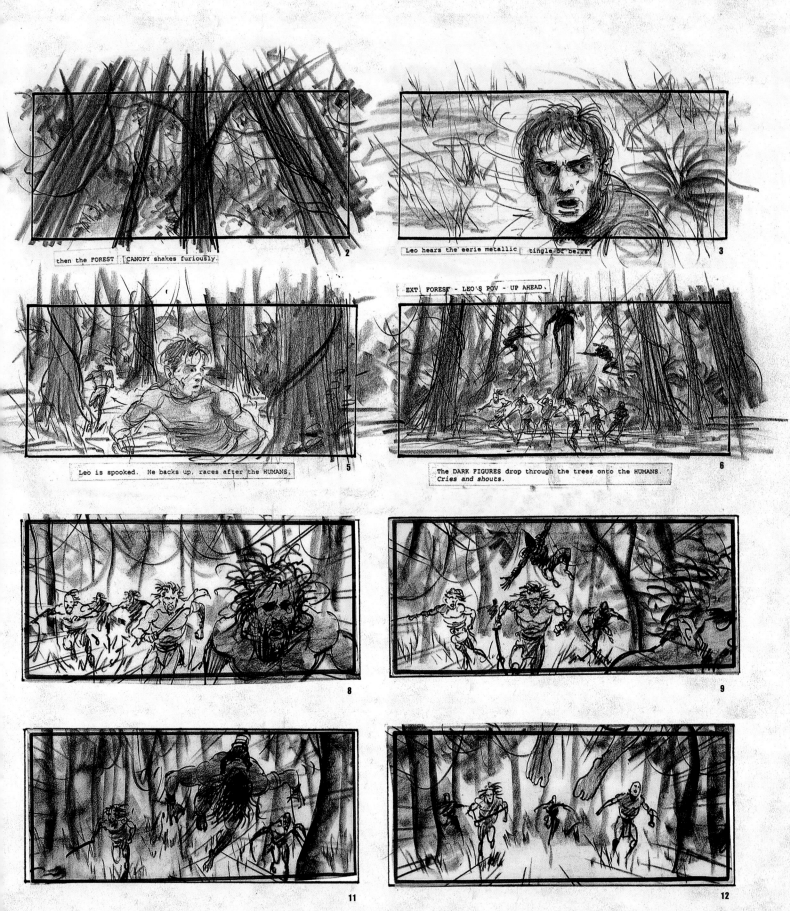

then the FOREST CANOPY shakes furiously. 2

Leo hears the eerie metallic tingle of bells. 3

Leo is spooked. He backs up, races after the HUMANS. 5

EXT FOREST - LEO'S POV - UP AHEAD.

The DARK FIGURES drop through the trees onto the HUMANS. Cries and shouts. 6

8

9

11

12

WRAPPING UP
IN STYLE

"This is a piece of **cinematic** history."

Executive Producer Ralph Winter

PRINCIPAL

PRINCIPAL photography on *Planet of the Apes* wrapped in March 2001, and with a late July release date, the postproduction team was facing a schedule just as daunting as preproduction had been. The bulk of the visual effects and sound work, as well as all the editing and final assembly, had to happen within 14 short weeks. As with every aspect of the film, the personnel involved were tops in their field and many of them Burton veterans—which didn't diminish the challenge but did ensure they would rise to it.

A large focus of attention at this stage was on completing the effects work and integrating it into the main photography. The production's point man coordinating this effort was visual effects producer Tom Peitzman, the key link between the producers (Burton, Zanuck, and Winter), the effects vendors (principally Industrial Light & Magic), and the editing team led by Chris Lebenzon. As Peitzman points out, this work actually began in preproduction, when he and the producers sat down with the script and prepared a complete effects breakdown, from which storyboard artists sketched each sequence involving effects work. Peitzman then took the breakdown and images to ILM to evaluate the work needed, estimate their costs, and put together their own in-house team and plan. ILM did 95 percent

of the effects work, Peitzman says, with other specialists brought in for some of the "practical" (as opposed to computer-generated) effects such as heavy wire- and rig-removal scenes—where the action is mechanically assisted by rigs that must then be erased from the final shot.

At ILM, visual effects supervisor Bill George headed the creative team, along with his co-supervisor George Murphy and producer Sandra Scott. By the time their work would be completed, in late June, they would have some 65 to 75 artists and technicians working on about 120 shots—everything from space travel to large crowd-replication shots. In all, the film uses around 300 FX shots. This sounds like a lot given that just a few years ago 200 was a high number for even the most effects-driven movie, but Peitzman and others emphasize a key difference between *Planet of the Apes* and truly CGI-dependent films

OPPOSITE: On the set at the Calima ruins. ABOVE: Concept art by ILM art director Jules Mann for the otherworldly skies over the Planet of the Apes. Ultimately, the moons were made larger and the solar light effects were downplayed. BELOW: Seven separate elements were meticulously composited by ILM compositors to turn 100 humans into 500.

BELOW: A blue-screen stage set with actors was combined with Hawaiian lava field footage and a miniature Ape City model—shot on the roof of ILM under moody skies—to create the escape from Ape City. BELOW: Storyboard sketch shows how close ILM's final composite was to the original concept for this shot.

ABOVE: Exterior shots of the *Oberon* space station were made using motion control photography over a detailed scale model that was later enhanced by adding CG structures and flying space pods. Details are added to the *Oberon* by ILM's model shop. It took a team of eight people two-and-a-half months to build the 13-foot-long, 120-pound structure, complete with working internal lights.

such as *The Mummy* or *Jurassic Park*. "We decided early on that we wanted a mostly 2D approach to depicting the apes in this film—that is, we would rely mainly on photographing real actors in makeup, masks, and costumes, rather than creating apes in the computer (3D) or with animatronics," says Peitzman. "Tim wanted to use physical elements, real people to make the shots come alive. And that's what's exciting about these characters: when they scream or roar or leap, you're seeing the real thing, not something created by a guy manipulating joysticks."

That said, the effects wizards at ILM had vital work to do on several key areas of the film. The space sequences near the beginning—Pericles the chimp in his flight simulator, the views outside the *Oberon*, Leo's and Pericles' pod flights, and the "wormhole" space disturbance that sucks Leo into the planet's gravity—were all created through various combinations of miniatures, matte paintings, and CGI work at ILM. The exterior of the *Oberon* also was a large-scale model built and photographed at ILM. Likewise, the jungle site where Leo's pod crashes began life as a very large miniature created at ILM, with the final shot incorporating live-action photography done on stage at LA Center Studios.

From space the effects work moved on to the environ-

ments of the planet itself. The Ape City was imagined as being built into the side of a mountain. The vast physical set that Rick Heinrichs's crew built on a Sony soundstage needed to appear within this larger landscape for long shots, so ILM built the mountain in miniature and seamlessly blended images of the full-size set into it (bringing the mountain to Tim Burton?). At one story point, the rebel humans and their ape friends return to the jungle locale where Leo crashed, finding it extensively charred from the heat of his re-entry—an effect realized with set extensions, miniatures, and matte painting, allowing Burton maximum flexibility to portray the environment in a wide-open way. Even the sky over the apes' planet called for some ILM magic, with its multiple moons and suns.

The massive battle scene near the end of the film brought both the story and the visual effects work to a climax. "Essentially," says Tom Peitzman, "we took 150 'real' apes and

FAR LEFT: Mauro Borrelli's concept art for the approach to Ape City. LEFT: ILM modelers Richard Miller and Danny Wagner work on the foam sculpture of the miniature Ape City. BELOW INSET: The seven-foot-long miniature sported dozens of tiny trees and vines. The ILM parking lot was used for lighting tests. BOTTOM: The finished shot integrated the Ape City miniature photography, digital matte painting and atmospherics, with a live-action plate of captured humans and ape soldiers photographed in the lava fields of Hawaii.

made them into thousands marching across the plains near Calima, through a process called tiling. And we multiplied the human forces as well. To give realism to the grand scale of these scenes, costumed actors were shot both on location in the desert and on special wire rigs in front of blue screens at LA Center, where a motion control rig was used to re-create the original motion of the location cameras. Back at ILM, the actors in each image tile would be stitched together, with extensive help from detailed hand-drawn masks, to create the illusion of a single event. The final blending includes additional dust elements shot at ILM, to match the atmospheric look of non-effects battle shots.

As the VFX shots were put together, all the parties involved could confer on them via satellite. Film editor Chris Lebenzon was based in New York, with Burton joining him there, while ILM is headquartered north of San Francisco. "I'll fly up to ILM or to New York once a week," describes Peitzman, "and we'll have a two-way satellite transmission where we can all see the shot and each other, and talk about what needs to be done. Tim even has an electronic pointer so he can put an arrow anywhere and explain exactly what he wants. It's an incredible tool, especially for this kind of accelerated postproduction schedule." When Burton returned to Los Angeles, teleconferencing with ILM would resume from that location.

Peitzman, who has done visual effects production for *Bedazzled*, *Inspector Gadget*, *Spawn*, and other films, echoes his colleagues on *Planet* in saying that the chance to be part of Burton's creative team was the most exciting part for him. "A lot of my job was making sure the look of the VFX shots is consistent with Tim's overall vision. That's what energizes me most: coming up with fresh concepts for a story we all loved as kids. Tim puts his personal stamp on movies in every detail, including the effects, so we tried hard to make them stylistically original—for example, a different vision of outer space than we've seen before."

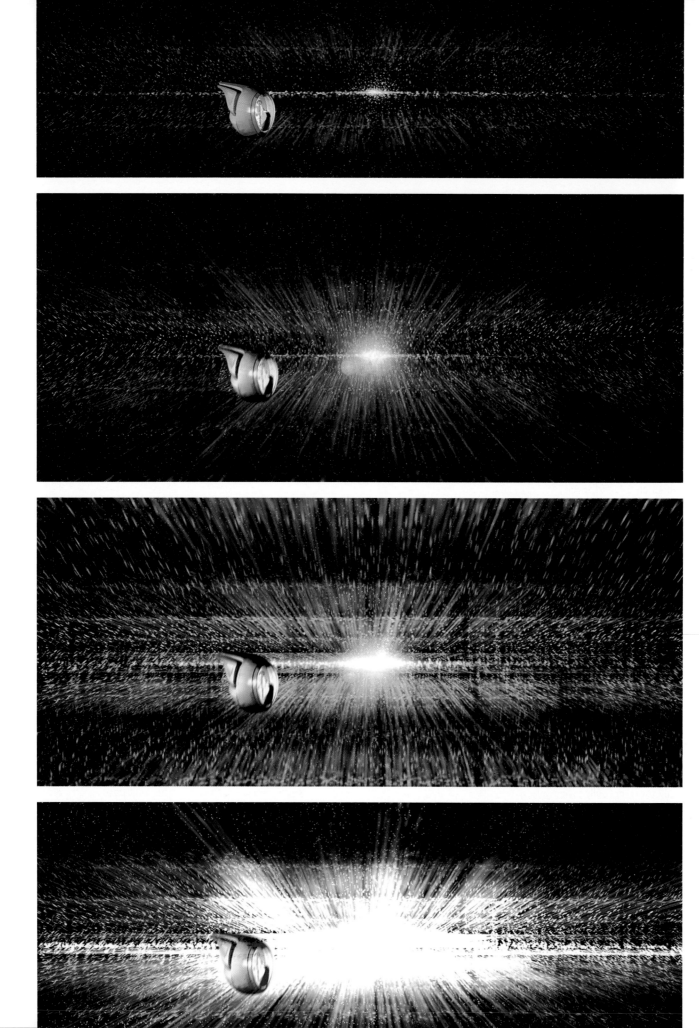

leaving the planet

THE denouement of the original *Planet of the Apes* remains one of the most startling of all time, and the makers of the new film found themselves in the unenviable position of trying to top it. "The questions in every interview," admits executive producer Ralph Winter, "are: Who's playing the Charlton Heston role? Is it a remake? and What's the ending? It could be irritating, but it's not. Those are things people remember about the first movie, the things they're interested in. We're interested in them, too, and we want to deliver something that's just as satisfying if not more so.

"It's clear that the ending of the first movie works on a lot of levels," Winter continues. "The original ending was perfect for that story, but ours is very different in its structure and themes and the arc of the characters—you can't really make an apples-and-apples comparison. It's hard to beat the iconic nature of the Statue of Liberty, so the bar is set very high. Tim struggled for a long time to come up with an equally strong idea, and I think we have—something that's concise and that does the same thing—turns the movie on its head so when you think you're safe, you're not safe any more."

The secrecy involved in the new ending was National Security tight. It wasn't attached to any copy of the script, and only those actually involved in the scene were given the script pages on the day it was shot. "We've tried to be very secretive," says Winter. "There's no script and very few storyboards have been drawn, which makes it difficult to prep and execute expediently." Indeed, even the creative heads for costumes, effects, and the like didn't know what the ending would be until a few weeks before the end of principal photography, then had to take a deep breath and scramble to gear up for it. "But we think the surprise is part of what people will enjoy when they see the movie," adds Winter. "We've left it a mystery so you don't feel like you saw the movie when you saw the trailer."

While the ending will remain a mystery until the day of release, what's never been in doubt has been the time, money, effort, talent, and above all passion that's been directed toward making this movie the best *Planet of the Apes* film yet. "It's going to be a visual treat," states second unit director Andy Armstrong. "There are so many talented artists involved. Of course it will be visually interesting, but we're all hoping it really draws people in because of the story. They're going to see a *Planet of the Apes* they haven't seen before."

The thrill of reimagining an old favorite is a frequent refrain. "I was fascinated with *Planet of the Apes* when I was a kid, and we're being allowed to take something we knew was really cool then, and try to make it better," enthuses stunt coordinator Charlie Croughwell. "From where I'm sitting it's the most exciting movie to come around in a long time," says Mark Wahlberg. "Something that's very intelligent and also very entertaining. I haven't been this excited in a long time."

Richard Zanuck, for one, doesn't believe that any fans of the original movie will be disappointed in what Burton and company have produced with this new version. "It's a franchise that has screamed out to be re-envisioned. It's amazing how long that basic idea has endured in our imagination, and there's still an attraction. We hit some kind of a nerve the first time about the relationship between man and ape, and did it in a way that still resonates. It was thought-provoking. I think we do the same thing here."

OPPOSITE: ILM's wormhole.
ABOVE: Pericles gives a thumbs-up.

THE SCREENPLAY

"The **little ones** make wonderful **pets**..."

Limbo, the orangutan slave trader

FADE IN:

EXT. SPACE

SPEEDING through star-spangled blackness. Infinity around us. Eternity before, and after.

INTO FRAME: Jupiter. A massive swirl of colors. Filling the screen for a beat.

CONTINUE PAST THE PLANET: as Jupiter's moons come into view, forming a breathtaking line of frozen orbs.

CHANGE DIRECTION with gut-wrenching speed. Looping closer to one moon.

PULL BACK past the metallic frame of what seems to be a ship's window to a multicolored control panel. Aglow with LCD lights.

INTO FRAME

a long, fur-covered finger punches buttons on the board. In a precise series. A course is digitally imaged.

TILT AND REVEAL: the *startling* vision of a CHIMPANZEE at the controls. Fitted with monitoring helmet and vest. His deep brown eyes sentient, intense.

A red light suddenly FLASHES on the panel. A *BEEP* sounds harshly. The chimp (PERICLES) quickly re-enters his command sequence. The *BEEP* gets faster. And the faster it gets, the more flustered he gets.

INT. FLIGHT SIMULATOR – CONTINUOUS

Through the window the LIGHT begins to fill the frame. Pericles tries to shield his eyes; now he can't see the BUTTONS on the board. Begins to SLAP at the controls in confusion.

The *BEEP* turns into one long wail. The view in the window freezes. The control panel goes black.

Reflected on the control panel — a second face — *human*. CAPTAIN

LEO DAVIDSON (20's) reaches over the chimp and punches off the beeping red light. Silence.

> **LEO**
> You lose.

WIDEN: *OBERON* – **REVEAL FLIGHT SIMULATOR**

PERICLES, the chimpanzee, vocalizes.

> **LEO**
> Surprised? I changed your flight sequence.

Pericles taps the keys. Confused. He looks to Leo.

> **LEO** (cont'd)
> I know you can hit the fast ball ... but what about the curve?

Pericles bangs the equipment hard like a toddler.

> **LEO** (cont'd)
> That's enough, Pericles.

Pericles starts to throw a small tantrum.

> **LEO** (cont'd)
> Stop it.
> (when he doesn't)
> ...or no treat.

Pericles stops *immediately*.

> **LEO** (cont'd)
> How well do I know you?

EXT. SPACE – OBERON

MOVING through the silence of space.

CARD: *JOINT FORCES MOBILE RESIDENT STATION, THE NEAR FUTURE*

INT. OBERON – CORRIDOR

ON THE WALL: a star-filled icon incorporating the AMERICAN FLAG, over which is written:

USAF OBERON

Leo walks quickly with Pericles. Pericles reaches up and takes Leo's hand.

EXT. OBERON – ANIMAL LIVING QUARTERS

Leo walks by a warning sign.

CAUTION: LIVE ANIMALS SECURITY ACCESS ONLY

INT. OBERON – ANIMAL LIVING QUARTERS

An EXPLOSION of animal noises as we sweep by cages of primates: mostly CHIMPANZEES, a few ORANGUTANS, GIBBONS, even a young lowland GORILLA.

Various med tech specialists work with the apes in the b.g: one specialist picks out a simple melody (easily recognizable) on an electronic keyboard for one ape; the ape watches, then tries to repeat the notes.

INSERT: The cages are marked with

metallic squares stamped with *SERIAL NUMBER* and *NICKNAME*.

Pericles scoots to the comforting arms of Chief Medical Officer LT. COL. GRACE ALEXANDER.

ALEXANDER
Was the *homo sapiens* mean to you again? (turns to Leo) We all know it's just rocket envy.

LEO
Ever consider an actual boyfriend?

ALEXANDER
You mean do I enjoy being miserable? I'll stick with my chimps.

Pericles jumps up on a counter. Pulls on a cabinet. Leo takes a biscuit from a huge bag of treats. Puts it behind his back, then holds out his hands. Pericles chooses right, nothing; left, not there either. Pericles *squawks*.

LEO
Another curve ball.

ALEXANDER
You weren't authorized to change his flight training.

LEO
I'm teaching him.

Leo pulls the biscuit from his back pocket. Hands it to Pericles.

ALEXANDER
You're teasing him.

LEO
He's gene-spliced, chromosome-enhanced ... a state of the art monkey ... he can take it.

ALEXANDER
When you frustrate them, they lose focus ... get confused. Even violent.

Across the room a CHIMP *screeches* and *rattles* its cage. Alexander brings Pericles over.

ALEXANDER (cont'd)
Congratulations, Pericles, you're going to be a daddy.

LEO
I thought I saw a smirk on his face.

ALEXANDER
Actually, the female was the aggressive one.

She looks right at Leo. Leo *reacts*. Is this a come on?

LEO
Aggressive works for me.

She looks up at him, smiles. A moment between them, then, a TECH appears.

TECH
Hey, Leo, you got a postcard.

NEW ANGLE

Leo takes the "postcard" — a small, thin wireless LCD monitor and finds a quiet place to sit by himself. Clicks on his mail. TIME CODE displays the date: **02-07-2029**

ON LCD SCREEN: EXT. LEO'S HOUSE — FRONT PORCH — DAY

Crammed in front of a lens, waving madly, are Leo's FATHER, MOTHER, SISTER, YOUNGER BROTHERS, and a few other relatives. A handsome, strong family. One little brother waves a toy model of the *Oberon*.

LEO'S MOTHER (flustered)
Now? OK. Hi, honey, it's me ... your mom.

Leo smiles warmly. His mother wears an *Oberon* pin on her dress. In the b.g. we can see a small old air strip with several planes, a hangar, and wind sock on a pole.

LEO'S MOTHER (cont'd)
I have so much to tell you ...

Leo's father steps forward in frame.

LEO'S FATHER
But she won't ... 'cause this is costing me a fortune. Hi, son. The TV showed some pictures of you from space.

The picture stutters. Jumps.

LEO'S FATHER (cont'd)
... we're all real proud of you ...

LEO'S MOTHER
... we just want you to come back to us safely ...

Her voice breaks. Leo *reacts*. Then the picture goes out. Leo bangs on the screen. It reads: *"YOUR SERVICE HAS BEEN INTERRUPTED."*

WIDER: The entire room goes dark for a moment. The animals *screech*. When the lights come back on, Leo rushes out.

INT. *OBERON* — JUST OUTSIDE BRIDGE

The security door. A shatter-proof glass barrier. LEO uses a **hand-print ID system** to gain access. The door slides open. Leo hurries through —

INT. *OBERON* — BRIDGE — CONTINUOUS

As LEO enters, crew members are gathered around a large digital screen. SPECIALIST HANSEN (20's) works the board with COMMANDER KARL VASICH (40's).

MAJORS FRANK SANTOS (30's) and MARIA COOPER (20's) are already there.

FRANK
We found it.

MARIA
It found us.

Leo looks up to see —

ON SCREEN: an electromagnetic cloud rushing through space

HANSEN
It's moving like a storm.

VASICH
That's what it is. An electro-magnetic storm ...

FRANK
This is what's causing blackouts on earth.

MARIA
It's ... beautiful.

VASICH
So's the sun til you get too close.

HANSEN
This is weird. I'm picking up frequency patterns.

VASICH
Tune them in.

ON SCREEN: A quick rush of images, including:

TV colors bars, digital grids, then a scene from *Bonanza*, a soccer game in Arabic, an old *American Bandstand*, the quiz show *Concentration*, Walter Cronkite, a cooking show, a Tom and Jerry cartoon, a BBC concert, the young Castro speechifying, *Ally McBeal*, public service spot in Spanish, Mao waving to the troops. All the while incongruous audio plays simultaneously: North Korean radio, pieces of cellular phone conversation, air pilot/tower chatter ... a ten-second montage of the history of world communication.

HANSEN
It's sucking up satellite relays, cell phone conversations, TV broadcasts ... every electronic communication from earth ... from all time.

LEO (sarcastic)
Ten billion channels and nothing to watch.

WIDEN

The ship goes dark again. A strange stillness settles over the bridge.

The power returns. The display has spooked them all.

MARIA
It sure knows how to get your attention.

VASICH
Let's get to work. We'll start with a pass through the core. Take initial radiation and gamma ray readings.

Vasich turns to Leo.

VASICH (cont'd)
Get your monkey ready.

Leo doesn't move. Looks at the other pilots.

LEO
Sir, this is a waste of time.

VASICH
We have standard procedures ...

LEO (over)
And by the time you go through all of them, it could be gone.

Vasich knows what Leo is lobbying for.

VASICH
No manned flights. First we send out an ape, then if it's safe, we send a pilot — in that order.

LEO
Let me do my job. You need somebody out there who can think, remember that? ... You need me.

Vasich is calm but firm.

VASICH
He's the canary. That's the coal mine. Alpha pod deploys at 1600.

CLOSE ON PERICLES: His soft brown eyes looking around anxiously for something. Finally focusing on — Leo.

WIDEN: INT. *OBERON* – LAUNCH PLATFORM

Alexander and her crew help Leo secure Pericles in the pod. Leo checks the flight suit. He tries to hide his concern from the chimp.

LEO
Just follow your sequence and then come home. Understand? Home.

The crew finishes up. Pericles vocalizes, looks for Leo — needing Leo's reassurance. Leo turns to Pericles, smiles, gives him a thumbs up.

PERICLES looks down at his own hand. Selects his thumb. Pulls it up — as the door is sealed and wipes screen.

INT. *OBERON* – FLIGHT CONTROL – DECK

Leo sits next to Vasich. Frank, Alexander, and the rest of the team huddle around. Through Leo's headset he hears an aural boilerplate of technical data.

ON THE DIGITAL SCREEN: Static pulses in brilliant colors

CLOSE ON control board

They watch the Apha pod trace the course of an ellipse around the *Oberon*. moving toward the energy cluster.

PUNCH EVEN CLOSER — the image of Alpha pod flickers.

Alexander leans forward.

ALEXANDER
What's wrong?

LEO
He's off course.

Vasich speaks in a dull monotone that obscures concern.

VASICH
Lock on him.

Leo slides forward a RED LEVER on the board. A beat, then —

LEO
He's not responding.

ALEXANDER
Surge in the heart rate. He's scared.

The MONITOR flashes, then goes dead. They're all stunned.

VASICH
Light him up again.

LEO
I can't ...

An endless second of frantic activity at the board. Frank checks his monitors.

CLOSER — on control board as the pod disappears.

LEO (cont'd)
Jesus. He's gone.

ALEXANDER
He's trained to come back to
the *Oberon.*

FRANK
If he's alive ...

PAN THEIR FACES — the silence is
agony. Leo can't just do nothing.

LEO
I'm waiting for orders, sir.

VASICH
We sit tight for now and wait.

Beat. Leo thinks.

LEO
I'll run some sequences in Delta
pod. See if I can figure out what he
did wrong.

Leo gets up and leaves.

INT. *OBERON* – LAUNCH PLATFORM –
DELTA POD – LATER

Leo sits into DELTA POD. Staring
out at the immensity of space. Over
the headset Leo can hear flight
control chatter.

ON SCREEN — Leo plots several
variations on Pericles' flight
sequences. Over the headset:
Leo recognizes Vasich's voice.

VASICH (OS)
OK, that's it. We lost him.

FRANK (OS)
Want to send another chimp?

PUSH IN CLOSE ON LEO — as he
waits for the response.

VASICH (OS)
No, it's too dangerous ...
shut it down.

WIDEN

Leo slowly swings his chair into
command position. His hand
trembles slightly as he reaches
for the pod door lock. Punches:
"LOCK." It seals with a hiss.

INT. *OBERON* – FLIGHT CONTROL –
DECK – LATER

Hansen reacts to something on flight
control. Checks his instruments,
then —

HANSEN (astonished)
Sir. Delta pod has launched.

VASICH rushes into frame.

INT. DELTA POD – SAME TIME

Leo leans back in his command
chair as a view of the *Oberon*
sweeps past the window behind
him. Leo squeezes into his gloves.
Takes control of the flight board.

EXT. SPACE – DELTA POD (MOVING)

Accelerating from the *Oberon*.

INT. DELTA POD – CLOSE ON LEO

IN SPACE. Vasich's voice sheds its monotone: full fury.

> **VASICH** (OS) (over radio)
> Delta pod, your flight is not authorized. Repeat, your flight is not authorized.

> **LEO**
> Never send a monkey to do a man's job.

> **VASICH** (OS)
> I swear you'll never fly again.

> **LEO**
> But I'm sure as hell flying now.

INTERCUT: FLIGHT DECK – SAME TIME

CLOSE ON HANSEN — looking at the digital screen.

> **HANSEN**
> I'm getting a Mayday, sir ... Jesus, it's on our secure channel ...

Vasich hurries over.

> **FRANK**
> Alpha pod?

> **HANSEN**
> I ... I don't know. But it's coming on strong.

> **VASICH**
> Put it up.

TILT UP TO DIGITAL SCREEN: *Out of the static figures emerge. In quick flashes. Jumpy, shadowed. Hard to read. Audio out of sync. We hear bits and pieces.*

> **VOICES** (filtered)
> ... help us ... massive turbulence ... request instructions ...

A loud wash of static and then silence.

The crew is stunned. Vasich lunges for the radio.

> **VASICH**
> Delta pod ... abort mission. Repeat. Delta pod ... return to ship ...

EXT. SPACE/INT. DELTA POD – LEO'S POV

as he follows Pericles' course around the *Oberon*. Vasich's voice melts into a rush of radio static.

FROM THE RIGHT — SWEEPING ACROSS SPACE

A tsunami of light washes through. Glittering particles. When it clears, Pericles' pod appears again.

> **LEO**
> *Oberon*. I've got a visual on Alpha pod ... Over.

All he gets back is another wash of static. He sets course for Alpha pod.

Another wave of light crests and falls. Alpha pod disappears. Leo has no way to process what he's just seen.

> **LEO** (cont'd)
> ... *Oberon?* Come back ...

For the first time we hear a note of fear in his voice. Leo twists in his seat to look out the side window.

LEO'S POV — RUSHING AT CAMERA

Another tidal wave of light — so thick it seems viscous. Leo braces himself. It rocks the pod as it sweeps by. Shakes Leo viciously.

INT. DELTA POD – CONTINUOUS

Then stops cold. Leo's control monitor goes black. All systems shut down. Leo bangs on the controls. In full panic.

EXT. POD – FROM SPACE

Powerless. It begins to drift, then pitch and tumble with increasing speed.

INT. POD

Leo's life support is down. He gasps for air.

> **LEO**
> *Oberon* ... Come in, *Oberon* ...

Leo flails at his helmet. It's a horrifying moment. He's almost unconscious.

EXT. POD – FROM SPACE/INT. DELTA POD – ANOTHER LIGHT WAVE

This one far bigger and brighter than before — rushes at the pod. Pummels it violently.

Leo's control monitor explodes into full color. Every system jumps back on.

INSERT DIGITAL DATE CLOCK: going haywire; it spins forward in time, then back in time. Then *shatters*.

LEO'S POV — THROUGH WINDOW

as the pod suddenly accelerates in a blur, pinning Leo back into his seat. Crushing him into his chair.

INT. DELTA POD – CONTINUOUS

BLACKNESS SWEEPS SCREEN

then gives way to a blue halo of light.

CLOSE ON LEO as he opens his eyes

(THE ENTIRE ENTRY ONTO THE PLANET IS SEEN FROM LEO'S POV.)

A wash of blues and purples — then the eerie, whistling rush that air makes as it generates friction on metal.

Leo looks down to see FLAMES licking the outside of the pod. The tiles on his heat shield are white. Smoke coats the cockpit with dark grease.

Leo tries to get his retros to fire — but the heat has disabled the control panel. He grabs a manual lever and fights to engage it. Engages.

INT. DELTA POD – LEO'S POV

The hazy outlines of land formations come rushing up at Leo. A huge expanse of dense green fills the pod window. Leo fights to recover some steering.

The shriek of the pod rises in pitch as it's about to impact with the surface.

Leo crashes through forest canopy and EXPLODES into water.

INT. DELTA POD — COCKPIT — UNDER WATER

Leo tries to fire open his entry door — the hinge has melted. Water pours in around him. He fumbles in the murky water for a red handle. His ejection seat control.

WIDEN

EXT. DELTA POD — UNDER WATER

as Leo trips his ejection seat — the cockpit door soundlessly explodes — sending a rage of bubbles at camera.

ACROSS FRAME — Leo is still strapped into his seat as he's thrust into the water like a torpedo.

Still underwater, Leo tears himself out of his flight suit and swims for the surface.

EXT. FOREST — BOG — SURFACE

Leo breaks free — gulps air. Swims for shore. Falls to his face — reeling.

EXT. FOREST — DAY

DISSOLVE THROUGH:

Close on Leo as his eyes open and his senses focus. He sits bolt upright.

LEO'S POV — 360-DEGREE PAN

Nothing but intense jungle. Leo stands, wobbly on his feet. Trying to get his bearings. Cut and bruised. Black grease from the fire streaked across his face. No idea where he is. He gets no time to think about it.

SOUND CUE: *Something is moving through the woods.*

Then Leo hears a frightening CRY. Leo's military training takes over. He moves quickly for cover.

EXT. FOREST — LEO'S POV (MOVING)

Racing through forest. Nettles rip his arms. He breaks from a tangle of vines. Stumbles over roots. *The sound is right behind him.* Leo wheels to fight. Picks up a stone.

ANGLE — BREAKING CLEAR

An older HUMAN (KARUBI), face decorated with intricate markings. He's carrying a sack of exotic fruits. Leo has no idea how to react — he cocks his arm with the stone.

ANGLE — BEHIND

Karubi's fierce YOUNG DAUGHTER (DAENA) appears —

DAENA
Father ... they're coming.

She knocks the STONE from Leo's hand. Karubi pushes Leo aside. Other humans appear — many with the same markings. Their raid on the fruit trees has become a run for their lives. Some are badly wounded. All following Karubi.

ANGLE

Leo is left alone. Looks around. Beat — then the forest canopy shakes furiously. Leo hears the eerie metallic tingle of bells. DARK FIGURES move with frightening speed toward him. Like ghosts.

Leo is spooked. He backs up, races after the humans.

EXT. FOREST — LEO'S POV — UP AHEAD

The dark figures drop through the trees onto the humans. Cries and shouts.

QUICK SHOTS: A human figure is suddenly propelled through the air — disappearing as it crashes in the underbrush. Branches snap. Loud cries seem to come from everywhere. A young human is dragged into the foliage.

Leo keeps moving. The nightmarish NOISE builds to an unbearable furor.

A hundred yards ahead the foliage clears. Giving way to a sun-drenched horizon. And hills in the distance. Karubi tries to lead the other humans that way.

Leo puts on a burst of speed. Hears a *growl*. Leo looks up.

EXT. FOREST

MATCH POV — Whatever it is looking down on Leo drops like a spirit through the trees. Branches whiz by. Leo grows in frame, until —

WIDEN

A ferocious GORILLA lands in front of Leo. Bares its canines.

CLOSER

The Gorilla wears armor across its massive chest and a strange helmet that glistens in the sun. This is ATTAR — the prodigious ape captain of the hunting party.

LEO
Jesus.

Leo grabs a branch to defend himself. Holds it like a spear.

ATTAR *reacts* almost with surprise. Then fury. With a fierce *growl* Attar snaps the branch in two. Hefts Leo into the air and hurls him. Leo *flies* backward. Hits the ground. Stunned.

Attar turns his attention to the other humans. He signals a line of gorillas behind him. High-pitched HORNS ring out.

EXT. FOREST — CONTINUOUS

ATTAR takes out a *bola* with heavy stones affixed to make it spin quickly. Whips it over his head — unleashes it.

The *bola* cuts the air with a frightening shriek. It catches a HUMAN MALE and wraps tightly around his legs.

TWO GORILLAS race forward and tie the captured human arms-overhead to long poles.

NEW ANGLE

MORE GORILLAS charge in from the other side with lightning speed. Dragging a long net affixed with hundreds of small bells; the apes shake it rhythmically — scaring the humans, driving them on.

NEW ANGLE

Other soldiers dash across the tree branches with incredible speed and balance, as if walking on air. They leap down on the terrified humans.

ON LEO

He staggers to his feet — starts to run. Looks over his shoulder. As the net closes in on Leo, he's able to fall into a small ditch and roll under it.

EXT. FOREST — FOLLOW LEO

He runs the other way. Cutting in front of him is a stocky human (GUNNAR) trying to flee with a LITTLE HUMAN GIRL (5) in his arms.

RACK FOCUS — BEHIND GUNNAR

Two gorillas chase him down. One gorilla plucks the child from his arms. The other gorilla knocks him forward. Apes swarm over him.

Karubi and Daena lead the humans through a stand of small saplings. The apes sweep across, ripping the trees out of the ground by their roots.

CLOSER ON KARUBI — breathing hard, afraid, listening closely.

But Attar attacks like a force of nature, graceful with his power, unrestrained with his speed. The humans in his way are overwhelmed. Only Karubi and Daena are left at large from this group.

NEW ANGLE: a slight BOY (BIRN, 15) eludes several apes. Feral and wild, he is very agile. But he doesn't see an ape hanging from a tree limb. The ape snags Birn with his feet. Wrenches him into the air.

KARUBI circles back to try to rescue

the boy. Two more apes drop down — slam him to his knees. Daena is bowled over. Karubi covers her with his body as a net envelops them.

EXT. FOREST — LEO

kneels behind a tree stump to catch his breath. Several apes drag human bodies away. Leo tries to take this all in.

An APE ON HORSEBACK crashes through the brush, dragging two humans behind. Leo waits til the ape rides by — then launches himself at the ape rider. Grabbing onto the reins, swinging himself up and knocking the ape off his mount.

Leo flips onto the horse. Tries to ride through the attack.

EXT. FOREST/LAVA TREE LINE — WIDEN TO NEW POV

Leo is suddenly plucked off the horse by an ape dangling from a tree. He's dropped hard to the ground.

POV — Leo looks up as Attar stands over him. Growls fiercely.

EXT. LAVA — ON THE EDGE OF THE FOREST — ROUND-UP CARTS

The clearing beyond the forest. Out of a haze of dust we see a dozen ornate CARTS with CAGES being loaded with humans. The carts are painted brightly with strange markings and symbols.

Attar is directing the loading of the carts. The humans are literally thrown inside. We see Daena tossed inside one cart. Then Gunnar, Birn. And finally, Karubi, who's been beaten severely.

FIND LEO

in a group of a dozen other humans. An ape binds Leo's hands tightly. Suddenly all the humans bow their heads, cower, turn their eyes to the ground.

LEO'S POV: the sun enshrouds a dark silhouette moving toward the captives.

Attar comes to attention — with obvious pride at the success of the hunt.

REVEAL an ape in a glittering gold uniform riding a massive black charger. This is THADE, general of the ape army.

Leo reads the reactions: a sense of glory from the apes; intense fear from the humans.

PUNCH CLOSE on Thade as he wheels his horse around and makes eye contact with Leo. Leo is the only human staring right at Thade.

Thade's reaction is lightning quick: in a blur he's off his horse and in front of Leo. Grabs Leo by the hair. In a fury.

THADE
This one looked at me.

CLOSE ON LEO: his bewilderment takes a new twist. *The ape spoke English.*

ATTAR
He won't do it again.

Leo reacts, grabs Attar by the wrist.

LEO (amazed)
You talk ...

ATTAR
Take your stinking hand off me, you damn, dirty human.

Attar swats Leo away — Leo is knocked unconscious.

DISSOLVE TO:

EXT. LAVA — ROAD TO CITY OF APES — CLOSE ON LEO

as he blinks awake. The carts are rolling on a road that winds into a hilltop city in the distance.

CRANE UP

as Attar rides in front of the caravan,

leading it into the CITY OF THE APES. The carts are pulled by young human males, each fixed with blinders.

LEO'S POV: EXT. CITY OF THE APES — DAY

A collage of old and new. Great stone buildings draped with bright tapestries, narrow streets and wide public spaces, busy with commerce and filled with apes.

Several old apes at a stone table argue over a game of chance. Several smoke from a pipe like a hookah.

A group of female apes haggle with a fruit vendor.

One young ape plays a long flutelike instrument for his friends. (This could be subtly evocative of the melody we heard on the *Oberon*.) A female ape passes by and drops a coin in his hat.

A chimp carves caricature-like human dolls out of wood. Another ape juggles using hands — and feet.

And in the most menial tasks we can see humans — carrying goods, pulling vehicles, chained. In all senses — *animals*.

PAN ACROSS

Most of the civilian apes ignore the carts.

Except for a group of young GORILLA KIDS who are playing a soccerlike game, using their prehensile feet to manipulate the ball. Several young

apes rush up and throw a volley of stones at Leo's cart.

INTO FRAME — a FEMALE CHIMP (ARI) rushes to stop them.

> **ARI**
> Stop it. You're being cruel ... Open your hands.

When the kids hesitate, she slaps their hands. The stones fall. Leo *reacts* —

> **ARI** (cont'd)
> Who told you you could throw stones at humans?

> **GORILLA KID**
> My father.

> **ARI**
> Then you're both wrong. And you can tell him I said so.

They run off. One gorilla kid turns and sticks out his tongue.

> **GORILLA KID**
> *Human lover.*

Ari scowls at him — they scurry away. NEW ANGLE as ARI's friend, another FEMALE CHIMP (LEETA), comes up.

> **LEETA**
> Do you always have to be so intense? I thought we're going shopping.

But Ari is staring as the carts pass her by. The humans wretched behind bars. CLOSER ON ARI — her eyes well with tears. Leo makes eye contact with Ari for one second.

Ari hurries after the carts.

> **LEETA** (cont'd)
> Ari ... You're going to get in trouble again.

EXT. CITY OF THE APES — CONTINUOUS — STAY ON THE CARTS

The other humans all keep their heads down. Silent. Leo looks at one human male, clearly dead. No one reacts to the body.

Leo catches the young boy, Birn, staring boldly at him. Through the layers of dirt Leo can sense his intelligence.

WIDEN

The CARTS suddenly veer to the side of the road. A procession of apes in what looks like monk's robes, faces wrapped in scarves, shuffle by in single file, chanting.

ATTAR moves toward the monks. They stop and give Attar their blessing. He bows his head, closes his eyes. We can sense his deep spirituality.

Leo crawls over to one human male, whose face is in his hand.

> **LEO** (whispers)
> Where am I?

He moves away from Leo. Leo tries a frightened human female.

> **LEO** (cont'd)
> ... What is this place?

CLOSER: the female looks quickly at Leo, eyes impossibly wide, too scared to speak. Then turns her face away.

INTO FRAME: KARUBI, pulls Leo back. Whispers urgently.

> **KARUBI**
> Head *down*. Mouth *shut*. You'll get us all killed.

Karubi looks around to make sure no ape has heard them. Daena glances at Leo. Leo decides he'd better bide his time. He kneels down with the others.

ATTAR shouts and the carts move on.

WIDEN: as the carts turn under a great stone arch.

CLOSE ON A HOODED FIGURE

happily slapping a small sap in his palm as he waits in the center of a walled quadrangle. LIMBO (ORANGUTAN) throws back his hood as —

EXT. APE CITY — LIMBO'S QUADRANGLE

The human carts come to a stop. Limbo strides forward. Looks over the humans. Turns to an ape soldier.

> **LIMBO**
> Are you trying to put me out of business? These are the skankiest, scabbiest, scuzziest humans I've ever seen.

> **APE SOLDIER**
> You don't want them?

> **LIMBO**
> I'll take the whole lot. I'll have to make it up on volume.

Limbo pays the soldier; turns to his handlers.

> **LIMBO** (cont'd)
> Get 'em out, get 'em cleaned!

Leo peeks up as the carts are overwhelmed by large gorilla handlers wearing germ prevention masks. It happens quickly: Cages thrown open. Humans dragged out. Men and women separated. Cries and shouts. The humans keep heads down.

Karubi has to be pulled away from Daena.

> **KARUBI** (quickly)
> Don't be afraid.

> **DAENA**
> I'll find you ...

Limbo appears IN FRAME suddenly.

> **LIMBO**
> Very touching. Really. I can't see for the tears in my eyes.

He drags Daena by the hair into the female pen. Karubi struggles to reach his daughter. One handler almost breaks his arm hurling him into the cage. Karubi shouts, collapses in pain.

Children are pulled from their mothers. Put in separate pens.

LEO is thrown into the male pen with Gunnar. Amazed at what's happening around him. Birn bites the hand of one handler. LIMBO appears — grabs Birn, shakes him hard, and tosses him in. Leo helps the boy to his feet.

> **LIMBO** (cont'd)
> How many times do I have to tell you? Wear your gloves when you handle humans.

> **THADE** (OS)
> Are you softening, Limbo?

LIMBO spins to see THADE — mounted, followed by ATTAR. Limbo turns from tyrant to toady in a second.

THADE (cont'd)
You used to hack off a limb.

LIMBO
Yes, General ... but unfortunately he's worth more intact.

Attar goes to the cage and spots Leo.

ATTAR
Don't turn your back on this one. He's feisty.

Karubi watches Leo closely. Limbo talks quickly, trying to suck up to Thade.

LIMBO
These the ones raiding the orchards, sir? I know an old country remedy that never fails. Gut one and string the carcass up ...

THADE
The human rights faction is already nipping at my heels.

LIMBO
Do-gooders. Who needs them? I'm all for free speech ... as long as they keep their mouths shut.

Thade stops by a pen with the human children. Wide-eyed, terrified. Thade looks them over.

THADE
I promised my niece a pet for her birthday.

LIMBO
Excellent. The little ones make wonderful pets ... but make sure you get rid of it by puberty. If there's one thing you don't want in your house it's a human teenager.

ON LEO: he watches a young ape and her ape mother walk over to the pen. Limbo quickly points out a few little girls.

LIMBO (cont'd)
Any one you want, sweetheart.

Like a kid in a pet store, the little ape looks over the children. Points at the 5-year-old girl we saw earlier.

LIMBO (cont'd)
Excellent choice.

Attar grabs the petrified LITTLE HUMAN GIRL and pets her head like a puppy — sets her in the little ape's arms. Her ape mother puts a leash on the human girl's neck as they leave.

IN THE FEMALE PEN — the little girl's human mother stares at the ground blankly. Her eyes dead.

Daena watches them take the little girl. We feel her rage.

Thade turns his horse to the gate. Limbo can't resist one last fawning word.

LIMBO (cont'd)
They say if you piss along the fence line it keeps them away from the crops.

THADE (stops him with a growl)
Close enough. You stink of humans.

He gallops off. LIMBO frowns, lifts his arm and sniffs.

EXT. LIMBO'S QUADRANGLE – ANOTHER ANGLE

As Thade and Attar ride off, we see Ari hiding behind the gate. Leeta is very nervous.

LEETA
No way I'm going in there. It's disgusting.

Ari isn't paying attention to her. She moves closer to the entrance.

ARI
What's disgusting is the way we treat humans. It demeans us as well as them.

Leeta grabs her hand.

LEETA
Ari ... we should go home.

ARI (snaps)
Then go home.

RETURN TO EXT. LIMBO'S QUADRANGLE

Leo moves round the PEN watching — not sure what's next.

LIMBO
Get 'em marked. I've got orders to fill.

Two handlers heft branding irons from a large stone fire pit.

LEO'S POV: They use poles with wire loops at the end to grab Daena by the neck. Drag her to a wooden post. Then the apes uncover her shoulders.

Karubi is enraged — shakes his cage.

KARUBI
No.

Limbo makes a funny face — pretends he's scared. Teasing Karubi. The other apes all laugh.

CLOSE ON DAENA: as the brand is pressed deep into her flesh. (The brand is faintly evocative of the icon from the *Oberon*.) But Daena does not scream. Her eyes burn with defiance. She's thrown back.

Two apes come for Leo. He digs his heels in but they easily drag him to the post. One handler quickly jabs the white hot iron. Leo twists himself and kicks it out of the ape's hand. Limbo is furious.

LIMBO
Do I have to do everything myself?

He reaches out to pick up the branding iron.

EXT. LIMBO'S QUADRANGLE – CONTINUOUS – WIDEN

Ari comes exploding into the quadrangle. She moves so quickly Limbo can't react at first. Opens a cage, knocks over a table, and finally grabs the branding iron and hurls it aside.

LIMBO
Oh, no, by Semos, not you again.

ARI
I cannot stand idly by while humans are being mistreated, tortured ...

Leo watches Ari. Karubi and the others rush to the bars.

Ari dashes past Limbo to the female pens. Turns the locks and throws open the gates. Before the women can escape, an ape handler appears — the women retreat back in the cage.

Limbo grabs Ari. She twists away.

LIMBO
The only reason I put up with your nonsense is because of your father.

ARI
If you want me to stop, give up your bloody business.

ON LEO: watching Ari carefully.

LIMBO
Hey, I do the job nobody else wants. I don't see any of you bleeding hearts spending all day with these dangerous, dirty, dumb beasts ...

ARI
They're not dumb. They can be taught to live with us ... and I'm going to prove it.

Leo reaches out for a chain snaked in the dirt — suddenly whips it around the foot of his handler. Yanks him off balance. His spear flies from his hand. Leo grabs it. Points it right at Ari's neck.

LIMBO
There's your "proof." Now I'll have to put him down.

Karubi and Daena watch intently.

WIDEN

Leo wraps an arm around Ari; tries to maneuver her to the gate. The handlers surround them. Offering a low growl. Leo looks over at the gate. He knows he won't make it.

CLOSER: Leo locks eyes with Ari. Ari is thrown by the intimacy of this act. No human has ever dared look her in the eyes this way. Leo leans inside the "space" between human and ape. He speaks intensely.

LEO
Please ... help me.

Ari is startled, frozen.

ANGLE

Daena realizes the handlers have been distracted by Leo. The door to the female pen is still open. She suddenly breaks out and runs for the gate. Limbo knocks her down hard. Turns furiously to Ari.

LIMBO
Look what you've started. Now I'm getting a headache.

Leo starts to back up, pressing the spear to Ari's neck.

LEO
Get back.

Limbo raises his hands, as if he's scared.

LIMBO
Oh, please, please don't hurt her.

Leo keeps his eyes on Limbo's hands — and doesn't see Limbo use his foot to reach up and grab the spear. In one second he wallops Leo. Stands over him.

LIMBO (cont'd)
Who needs this aggravation? Hold him.

Limbo hefts the spear. Ari makes her choice —

ARI
Sell him to me.

LIMBO
Are you crazy? He's wild ...
(re: Daena)
... they're both wild.

ARI
Then I'll buy them both.

Limbo freezes — a look comes over his face. Nothing gets his attention like money. Leo and Daena exchange a look.

LIMBO
That would be expensive ... very expensive.

ARI
I'm sure we could come to a deal.

Limbo scratches his head. He can't resist.

ARI (cont'd)
Deliver them to my house.

LIMBO
I'll have to mark him first.

In one quick thrust Limbo brands Leo.

WIDE SHOT: EXT. CITY OF THE APES – NIGHT

The evening darkens as the moons rise above the city.

EXT. ARI'S HOUSE – NIGHT

High-walled gardens strung with red lanterns. Tapestries billow in the night breeze. We hear loud voices.

ARI (OS)
Father, please, I'll pay with my own money.

INT. ARI'S KITCHEN – NIGHT

Ari chases her father (SANDAR, chimpanzee, hair streaked with gray) into the kitchen.

SANDAR
Your "own money" is going to make a pauper of me ... Where are they?

KRULL (a large, elder silverback Gorilla) points. On the other side of the room Leo and Daena kneel on the floor with TWO OTHER HUMANS (TIVAL and BON). Sandar groans when he sees them.

Tival and Bon rise immediately. These "house humans" are well-groomed, wear nice robes.

KRULL (to Leo and Daena)
Rise when your master enters.

Daena scowls — doesn't move. Krull yanks her up. Leo stands and faces the old chimp.

SANDAR
Semos help me, wild humans in my house.

ARI (re: Leo)
This one seems different.

SANDAR (dismissive)
How different could he be? You can't tell one from the other.

Leo looks up at Ari, meets her eyes again. Looking right at her. She is flustered, turns away.

They hear the sound of voices O.S. Sandar is flustered.

SANDAR (cont'd)
My guests are here. Keep the savage ones out of sight ... especially from General Thade.

Ari *reacts* —

ARI
Father ...

SANDAR
And you'd better be nice to him.

Sandar runs out. Ari looks at Leo — runs after her father.

EXT. ARI'S DINING PATIO – NIGHT

A long table and garlands of fruit and flowers. A party of apes engages in small talk.

AT THE FRONT DOOR

Sandar exchanges ape touches with SENATOR NADO (an elderly ORANGUTAN) and his wife NOVA (a young CHIMP).

SANDAR
Good evening, Senator Nado, you look lovely tonight.

NOVA
I'm having a bad hair day.

She sighs and strokes the fur on her face.

NADO (rolls his eyes)
Yet she spends a fortune grooming herself.

NOVA
And I'm worth every penny.

She strokes her old husband quickly and runs ahead of him inside.

FIND ARI WITH LEETA: in elegant embroidered robes.

LEETA
Thade is powerful and aggressive ... what else could you want in a male?

ARI
Someone I can respect ... and who respects me.

LEETA
Don't play so hard to get. Say yes to him and you'll be invited to every exclusive party in the city.

ARI
How many silly parties can you go to?

LEETA
How many are there?

KRULL appears ringing a small bell. Sandar sweeps through.

SANDAR
Please, everyone, sit.

INT. ARI'S KITCHEN – SAME TIME

At the sound of the bell Tival and Bon carry wooden trays of food upstairs. As soon as they leave Leo jumps up, tests a window with wooden shutters. Won't budge. Leo turns to Daena.

LEO
How the hell did these monkeys get this way?

Daena just stares —

DAENA
What other way would they be?

LEO
They'd be begging me for a treat.

DAENA (confused, looks at him)
What tribe do you come from?

LEO
It's called the United States Air Force. And I'm going back to it.

Krull suddenly appears.

KRULL
Finish your work ... no talking.

Krull grabs another tray of food and leaves. Leo waits, then picks up a tray — peeks up the stairs.

EXT. ARI'S DINING PATIO

The apes are seated at a long table. Sandar at the head. Ari across from Leeta. The chair next to Ari is still open.

NADO
We just returned from our country house in the rain forest.

Krull offers food to each guest.

SANDAR
And how was it?

NOVA
Bor-ing.

NADO
I find it relaxing ... being away from the frantic pace of the city.

NOVA
I wanted to go out. But there was no place to go ... nothing but trees and rocks. All you did was nap.

133

NADO
Exactly. A bit of time away from politics is what is needed for a weary soul like me.

ON LEETA AND ARI whispering.

ARI
Look at the old fool ... he left his wife and children for her ... a chimp half his age. Now he can't keep up.

LEETA
But he's worth a fortune.

BACK TO NADO

He reaches for Sandar. Gives him a gentle touch.

NADO
We used to lose ourselves for days in the forest when we were young. Now I can barely climb a tree.

SANDAR
It's trite but true. Youth is wasted on the young. Now that I have so much to do ... I'm exhausted ... Still, some nights I dream of hurtling through the branches ...
(sighs)
How did I get so old so fast?

THADE (OS)
Living with your daughter would age any ape quickly.

They all turn as THADE enters the party with ATTAR.

ARI
Quick. Switch seats.

LEETA
No, he's here to see you.

Thade waits for Krull to pull out the chair. Krull doesn't move. Attar hurries to hold the chair for Thade. We can sense enormous hostility between Thade and Krull.

Thade sits next to Ari. Sandar shoots Ari a look which says, "Please don't be rude."

SANDAR
You are too long a stranger in our house.

THADE
My apologies, Senator. I stopped to see my father.

SANDAR
How is my old friend doing?

THADE
I'm afraid he's slipping. I wish I could spend more time with him ... but these are troubled times. Humans infest the provinces ...

ARI
Because our cities encroach on their habitat.

THADE
They breed quickly while we grow soft with our affluence. Even now they outnumber us ten to one.

NOVA
Why can't the government simply sterilize them all?

NADO
The cost would be prohibitive ... Although our scientists do tell me the humans carry terrible diseases.

ARI
How would we know? The army burns the bodies before they can be examined ...

Ari turns to Sandar for support.

ARI (cont'd)
Father.

SANDAR
At times, perhaps, the Senate feels the army has been a tad ... extreme ...

THADE
Extremism in defense of apes is no vice.

Senator Nado is about to bite into a piece of fruit. Attar *growls* — they all freeze. Attar closes his eyes and prays.

ATTAR
We give thanks to you, Semos, for the fruit of the land. Bless us, Holy Father, who created all Apes in his image. Hasten the day when you will return ... and bring peace to your children. Amen.

All the guests quickly say "Amen." Attar looks over at Krull, uncomfortable under the glare of the old silverback.

INT. AT THE TOP OF THE STAIRS

LEO is looking for a way out when an ape soldier sees him and pushes him into the —

EXT. ARI'S DINING PATIO

Thade notices LEO enter the room. Leo has no choice but to pretend to serve. He tries to hide his face from Thade. Thade sees Leo serving from the tray.

THADE
What is this beast doing in your house?

Ari exchanges a look with her father.

ARI
He'll be trained as a domestic.

THADE
Your ideas threaten our prosperity. The human problem will not be solved by throwing money at it. The government tried once and all we got was a welfare state that nearly bankrupted us.

ATTAR
And changed the face of the city.

LEETA
I think the city has about as much diversity as I can handle.

Ari glares at Leeta. She holds up her embroidered scarf.

ARI
This garment was made by one of my humans.

Ari smiles at BON, who averts her eyes nervously.

ARI (cont'd)
Can you deny the skill? Isn't it obvious they are capable of a real culture?

THADE
Everything in "human culture" takes place below the waist.

The guests all laugh.

NADO
Next you'll be telling us that these beasts have a soul.

ARI
Of course they do.

ATTAR
The senator's daughter flirts with blasphemy.

Thade and Attar exchange a look. Thade grabs Leo powerfully. Knocking the tray and its food to the floor.

THADE
Tell me. Is there a soul inside you?

CLOSE ON LEO — on the floor. He sweeps up the food. EVEN CLOSER: on a small prong the apes use as a fork. Leo slips it into his shirt. Thade pushes Leo away. Holds his hands up with disgust.

THADE (cont'd)
Quick, a towel ...

The guests all laugh at Leo. Ari's had enough. She stands.

ARI
You're all cruel and petty ... and I've lost my appetite.

A quiet embarrassment in the room as Ari storms away from the table.

Sandar seems embarrassed — he gestures to Thade: Go after her.

INT. ARI'S BEDROOM/EXT. ARI'S BALCONY — NIGHT

The room is dark; Ari lights a candle

INSERT: AN ICON: an ape (SEMOS) with a golden penumbra round his head. Floating down from the clouds.

Ari finds solace as she settles among her collection of "human artifacts" — human dolls and crafts.

CLOSER: Ari senses his presence first; Thade steps out of the shadows.

THADE
I have no patience for these society dinners ... I only came to see you.

Ari cuts him off.

ARI
Then you've wasted your time.

Thade moves quietly to her. Begins to touch her fur softly, somewhere between apelike grooming and a lover's caress. Ari tries to pull away. Thade grips her strongly with his hand. He nuzzles her neck.

THADE
My feelings haven't changed ... you know how much I care for you.

ARI
You only "care" about my father's influence ... and your own ambition.

Ari pulls away. Thade flashes his canines, snarls —

THADE
I know about the trouble you caused today. I could have you arrested ...

Ari won't back down.

ARI
What I did was right. I'd do it again.

THADE
You feel so much for the humans ... yet can't feel anything for me.

He leaves.

EXT. ARI'S HOUSE — NIGHT

Attar waits as Thade mounts his horse.

ATTAR
A moment, sir.

Thade is lost in thought. Looks at Ari's scarf in his hands.

ATTAR (cont'd)
It's important.

THADE (darkly)
What is it?

Attar motions — two ape soldiers come out of the shadows. Nervous before Thade.

135

ATTAR
These men insist on speaking to you. They won't tell me what it's about.

EXT. CITY OF THE APES — NIGHT

A perfect stillness settles over the city.

INT. ARI'S KITCHEN — NIGHT

Krull locks Leo, Daena, Tival, and Bon behind a cage door. Leaves. Bon immediately curls up on a floor blanket.

CLOSER ON LEO — he slips out the PRONG. Goes to the LOCK. Reaches his arm through the cage. Begins to work the lock.

Daena comes closer — watching Leo work. The lock is old — Leo hears the click — then jerks it free. Throws open the door. Daena follows him out. Tival and Bon don't move.

BON
There's a curfew for humans.

TIVAL
If you're found on the street at night ... they'll kill you on sight.

LEO
If you stay here ... you're already dead.

Tival hesitates, then steps out. Bon retreats back farther.

BON
Our mistress has been so kind to us.

DAENA
She's your enemy.

Bon sinks deep into the cage, unable to leave. Leo rifles through the kitchen utensils. Finds a knife.

LEO (to Daena)
Can you lead me back to the place where they caught us?

Daena nods. Leo hurries her toward the door.

DAENA
Not without my father.

LEO
Too dangerous. We have to go right now.

Daena pulls away. Defiant.

LEO (cont'd)
You don't have a clue who I am. Or where I'm from. And you wouldn't understand if I told you. But I can help you.

DAENA
Find your own way back.

Leo *reacts* — she's tougher than he thought.

EXT. FOREST — BOG — NIGHT

The woods are moon bright. Thade rides behind the two ape soldiers. Just skirting the bog.

FIRST APE SOLDIER
Here! This is where I saw it.

Thade dismounts.

THADE
Go on.

SECOND APE SOLDIER
Something fell from the sky.

FIRST APE SOLDIER
With wings of fire.

SECOND APE SOLDIER
There was a terrible thunder and the ground itself shook! I thought we'd all be killed.

The apes look at each other nervously.

THADE
Are you sure you didn't dream this?

FIRST APE SOLDIER
It was no dream, sir. Look!

ON THADE: as they come upon the charred and broken trees like skeletons in the moonlight.

THADE
Who else did you tell?

FIRST APE SOLDIER
No one, sir. We knew we had to come right to you.

CLOSE ON THADE: as he sets his hands on their shoulders.

THADE
You did exactly the right thing.

CLOSE ON A BOWL OF FLOWERS: bright, fragrant blossoms. A FURRY HAND comes into frame and crushes them with a stone pestle.

WIDEN AND REVEAL: INT. LIMBO'S HOUSE — NIGHT

Limbo stands in front of a large mirror. Looks himself over. Sniffs. Sighs. Then starts to rub the crushed flowers across his armpits and chest.

EXT. LIMBO'S QUADRANGLE — HUMAN PENS — NIGHT

Karubi rests with Gunnar. The young feral boy, Birn, looks out through the slats. POV — he's focused on a tiny slice of the night sky. As if it were a lifeline. Birn suddenly jumps up. He HEARS SOMETHING moving above him.

PUNCH CLOSE ON BIRN: his eyes alive, senses alert. Now Karubi hears it. Gestures for them to be quiet.

EXT. HUMAN PENS — SAME TIME

TWO of Limbo's GORILLAS walk past the pens. ONE GORILLA stops, looks up at the roofline, sniffs, cocks his head.

FIRST GORILLA
You smell that?

SECOND GORILLA
Don't start now. We're off duty. And I'm starvin'.

They leave. PAN UP TO THE ROOFLINE. A shadow moves.

INT. HUMAN PENS – THROUGH THE SLATS

A sound — then a SHADOW ripples past. Karubi recoils against the back wall. Looks for something to use as a weapon. Tears away a wooden plank. Prepares for an attack.

INTO FRAME

DAENA appears. Reaches out her hand. Karubi takes it. Kisses it. The gate suddenly *rattles*. CLOSER — a rope snakes through. Karubi hurries over and pushes the other end back outside.

ON LEO — outside the pen

Leo uses a stake to twist a strand of rope tighter until the slat snaps. They all freeze at the SOUND. Listen. No one has heard it. Daena and Tival pull back the gate. Birn is out first. Then Gunnar. Karubi comes out slowly. Daena sees his injured arm.

DAENA
You're hurt.

Karubi folds her into a warm embrace.

KARUBI
How did you get away?

Daena turns to Leo. Karubi gives Leo a long look over.

KARUBI (cont'd)
Who are you?

LEO
Just somebody trying to get the hell out of here.

Gunnar pokes at Tival.

GUNNAR
This is one of their house humans. He thinks he's better than us ...
(steps closer to taunt him)
He thinks he's part ape.

LEO (to Daena)
You promised to show me the way back.

Daena looks to Karubi.

KARUBI
We'll go together.

EXT. LIMBO'S QUADRANGLE – ON THE ROOF – NIGHT

Leo steps onto the rooftop. Followed by Karubi, Daena and the others. They move quickly. Silhouettes against the moon-bright sky. They know what will happen if they're caught.

EXT. ROOFTOPS – ANGLE – ON THE ROOF

FOUR TEENAGE APES pass around a JUG, all a little tipsy.

ONE TEENAGE APE
Shhh, I hear something.

SECOND TEENAGE APE
I think it's my mom. Hide it!

ONE TEENAGER runs to stash the jug. Comes face to face with LEO. He lunges for Leo but falls, too dizzy from the drink. Leo kicks open the ATTIC DOOR. The others race after him. The teenage apes *roar* loud enough for the alarm to carry.

INT. BUILDING

WIDEN as they rush into building.

They fly down stairs. Leo veers off through another door. Moving quickly they pass through:

INT. BEDROOM (CONTINUOUS)

NADO is in bed. NOVA comes out of the bathroom in a sexy short robe. Slinks into bed.

NOVA
Honey? I'm feeling frisky ...

SNORE ... Nado is fast asleep. She *growls* and snuggles up to him just as LEO and the OTHERS explode into the room. Nova lets out a *howl*. She jumps to the ceiling. A moment later Nado does the same. Leo veers for another door —

INT. APE APARTMENT (CONTINUOUS)

An OLD APE removes his wig, revealing a bald head — setting the wig on an ape bust. Then he takes out false teeth, sighs, puts them in a glass

as — Leo explodes through the door. Leo overturns the bust but never stops moving. Out the window, over a balcony. Through another window —

INT. BEDROOM (CONTINUOUS)

THADE'S NIECE (the LITTLE APE we saw earlier) is putting her "pet" to bed in a small CAGE. The human child's eyes are filled with tears.

Leo and Karubi burst into the bedroom. Daena sees the little girl — runs across the room and grabs her.

PUSH IN ECU as the little ape opens her mouth, revealing tiny canines, and starts to howl.

INT. LIMBO'S HOUSE — SAME TIME

Limbo picks off pieces of flower petals stuck all over his fur. He hears the ROARS outside. *Reacts.*

EXT. STREETS — NIGHT

Attar leads his soldiers through the city. Wait until they pass, then —

TILT UP TO ROOF

Leo hangs from an eave — then drops down into the street. Daena hands him the Little Girl. She drops next. Then Gunnar, Birn, Tival. Karubi can only use one arm — he FALLS from the eave. Hits hard. Daena runs to him.

KARUBI
Leave me ...

DAENA
No ...

KARUBI
I'm tired ... and just too old. And old men get scared.

LEO
You might be old and tired ... but you're done being scared.

Leo helps Karubi to his feet. Daena supports him.

GUNNAR
Apes.

EXT. STREETS — CONTINUOUS

Stepping out of the shadows: TWO APES. Leo pulls his knife. Prepares for the attack.

It's ARI. In a flash Krull disarms Leo. Ari is upset.

ARI
You're lucky I found you before they did. Come back with me to the house. I can reason with them.

KARUBI
I know how apes "reason."

BON, Ari's servant, stands meekly behind her. She looks quickly at Tival, then bows her head.

LEO
Is there another way out of the city?

Ari reacts. Leo can see it in her eyes right away — she knows something. Krull tries to stop her.

KRULL
Do not get involved with these humans.

Leo steps closer to Ari — it unnerves her. He speaks quickly, forcefully.

LEO
Why did you save me? Why'd you take the chance?

Ari is flustered, then —

ARI
I ... don't know. You are very unusual.

LEO
Like you can't even imagine. Come with me ... and I'll show you something that'll turn your whole world upside down.

DAENA (sharply to Leo)
So this ape will understand you but I can't?

CLOSE ON ARI — her mind racing. They can hear the howls of ape patrols echo across the city. Finally, Ari makes her decision.

ARI
When I was little I found a way to sneak outside the city walls. Where no one could find me. I can lead you there.

KRULL
If you are caught, even your father won't be able to protect you.

ARI
You know what the soldiers will do to them.

KRULL
Your father did not order it.

ARI
He didn't forbid it, either.

The old gorilla cannot refuse her. He looks them over.

KRULL
This human child cannot survive the journey.

ARI
My servant woman will hide her in my house.

Gunnar glares at Bon as she steps forward. Ari reaches for the little HUMAN GIRL. Daena steps back — can't bring herself to let go. Karubi surprises them all by taking the Little Girl from Daena. Karubi hands her to Ari. Bon moves off quickly, disappearing into the shadows. Ari looks at Leo, then runs off. The others follow quickly.

EXT. STREET — SAME TIME

Ari runs through the shadows with Leo leading the others. Down the long, narrow street. STAY ON KARUBI — in great pain. Watching carefully. The city seems alive. He knows the what the sounds signify: the apes are hunting them again.

WIDEN

They turn a corner.

KARUBI'S POV: at the far end of the street

Several DARK SHAPES appear. Krull quickly pulls Ari into the shadows.

PUNCH IN CLOSE — ATTAR

Too late. He sees Ari with the humans. Attar lets out a terrible roar.

KRULL
They've seen us.

CLOSE ON KARUBI: He touches Daena gently.

KARUBI
Hurry.

When she realizes what he's doing —

DAENA
No, Father ...

KARUBI
Don't worry. I'll be right beside you. Just like always.

Karubi dashes out of the shadows.

DAENA
Father.

EXT. IN THE STREET — FOLLOWING KARUBI

Karubi charges forward straight at Attar.

ON ATTAR: He flashes his canines at Karubi.

CLOSER — KARUBI running through his pain. He grabs a heavy wooden TOOL left by a doorway and wields it like a spear. With a warrior's cry Karubi attacks Attar.

ATTAR merely puts out his arm to deflect the blow. With dazzling power he hurls Karubi to the ground. Karubi lies stunned for a second. He pushes himself to his knees. Looks up to see Attar standing over him. Ape soldiers encircle him.

ATTAR
Why do you not tremble before me?

To Attar's dismay, a smile plays across Karubi's face as he recalls Leo's words.

KARUBI
I'm done being scared.

CLOSE ON ATTAR — surprised at the heroism of this human. The nobility in Karubi's eyes freezes him. He can't quite bring himself to kill him.

NEW ANGLE — The clatter of hoof-beats on stone. THADE charges into frame on his horse. Sword raised.

TILT UP to a shadow on the wall — as Thade's sword pierces Karubi. (OR: THADE leaps from his horse to kill Karubi with his hands.)

EXT. MOVING THROUGH THE SHADOWS — SAME TIME

Leo, Ari, Krull, Daena and the others HEAR the heart-rending last CRY of Karubi. Daena tries to break away to go to him. But Krull stands in her way like a stone wall. Daena struggles ineffectively against his strength. Krull hands her to Leo.

EXT. STREET

FOLLOW THADE charging back down the street with Attar and the soldiers.

THADE
Where are the other humans?

ATTAR
This way ... they can't have gone far.

AT THE END OF THE STREET

The soldiers fan out. But there is no sign of the humans. Attar sniffs the air, looks around, surprised.

ATTAR (cont'd)
They've disappeared.

THADE
Ring the city. Block every gate ... When you find them, kill them all. But keep the troublemaker alive. I must talk to him before he dies.

Attar hesitates; this is very hard for him to say.

ATTAR
Sir ... the Senator's daughter is with them.

Thade *reacts* —

THADE
They took her?

ATTAR
She is helping them. I saw her myself.

Thade is thrown by the news — but he recovers quickly and puts a "spin" on Ari's involvement.

THADE
She had no choice. She was terri-fied. They threatened her life. I will report the matter to the Senate myself.
(then)
They'll beat their chests and ask for my help.

ATTAR
They are weak without you, sir.

THADE
Has she taken the old silverback with her?

Attar is unhappy about the answer he must give.

ATTAR
Yes, sir.

THADE
I trust that will not be a problem for you.

Thade stares intensely at Attar.

ATTAR
No, sir — as of now he is a criminal.

But Attar is troubled.

WIDE SHOT: EXT. LAVA — NIGHT

An old stone CISTERN and SPRING HOUSE. The heavy wooden door shakes. Can't be moved. Suddenly it shatters. KRULL powers through — his old body still prodigiously strong compared to humans.

The humans stop to catch their breath. Last, Ari steps out. She sees Daena, face streaked with tears, staggered by her father's death.

ARI (gently)
Your father was a brave man.

Daena focuses her rage on Ari.

DAENA
You know nothing about my father.

Daena flies at Ari. With stunning speed Ari flashes her canines and slaps Daena to the ground. In a moment humans separate from apes. Krull *roars* and shields Ari — who's already regretting what she's done.

Leo helps Daena to her feet.

DAENA (cont'd)
Let ... me ... go.

She breaks free of Leo and runs off powerfully into the forest.

Ari looks back at the city — and the life she has put in jeopardy.

KRULL
Move quickly ... Thade will be after us.

Krull turns to close up the tunnel door by moving a massive rock in its place.

Ari and Leo run off.

STAY WITH Leo and Ari.

LEO
He's no servant.

ARI
Krull was a general ... til he opposed Thade. Thade ruined his career ... My father took him in.

LEO
I'm glad he's on our side.

WIDEN: EXT. FOREST — NIGHT

Impossibly lush. MOVING ACROSS FRAME: DARK SHAPES in a blur.

REVEAL: Daena leads the way — running like a deer through the thick foliage. Leo racing after her. Leo hears something right behind him: BIRN continues to be his shadow. Birn smiles at Leo. Leo doesn't want to deal with him.

WIDEN

ARI streaks past them all easily. She looks back to make sure Leo can see her. Leo and the other humans stop to catch their breaths. Ari lopes back, hardly winded. Tival immediately offers her fruit and water. Daena and Gunnar watch.

GUNNAR
Look how they pamper her.

Ari hears them, pushes the food away.

ARI
I'm fine.

DAENA
Apes are always fine ... as long as you have humans to serve you.

Leo looks back to see if they're being followed.

LEO
Keep moving.

They start off again. Krull stops Leo.

KRULL
If this is some human trick, I will kill you.

EXT. BACK TO THE STONE CISTERN

at the end of the hidden tunnel. A SHADOW moves. We can just make out two YELLOW EYES.

Someone is following them.

DISSOLVE THROUGH:

EXT. FOREST — DAWN

TWO SUNS take their place as the first violet streaks of dawn appear.

EXT. BOG — DAWN

The stippled pale light is reflected in deep still water.

CLOSER — in the water

LEO'S REFLECTION appears. TILT UP and find Leo — racing along the bank. He's wound up with the adrenaline of hope.

INTO FRAME: The others try to keep up with Leo — then they stop, astonished at the sight.

POV — BURNT TREETOPS mark a charred trajectory from the sky into the forest where Leo crash-landed. It's unmistakable that something powerful went into the water.

LEO
This is where I flew in ...

Ari and Krull are not sure what to make of all this. The others are confused and unsettled by this startling image.

ARI
You caused this?

LEO
My retro-burners ...

Birn's eyes are wide. Leo's excitement infects him. Gunnar pushes forward to Daena. He won't admit it — he's spooked.

GUNNAR
The soldiers will be hunting us. We can still make it to the mountains.

Daena touches a scarred tree.

DAENA
I don't understand. You fell from the sky?

LEO
With my ass on fire.

Krull gives Ari a very skeptical look.

ARI
I'm sure he'll explain everything.

KRULL
How can you explain what can't exist?

LEO
I'll tell you what "can't exist." You. Talking monkeys. This whole place.

Leo traces a streak of black soot leading deeper into the bog. Krull stops Ari from following.

LEO (cont'd)
What's wrong?

ARI
Apes cannot swim. We will drown in deep water.

Daena glares at Ari.

DAENA
That's why we pray for rain every day.

But Ari follows Leo anyway. Leo spots an OIL SLICK.

LEO
There's where I went in.

Before they can *react* — Leo dives into the bog and disappears beneath the water.

ON THE BANK: the others wait. No idea what to think. Birn stands on the edge. The silence unsettles them. No sign of Leo. Finally, Ari looks at Daena —

ARI
How long can a human hold his breath beneath the water?

Birn looks at Deana — is Leo in trouble? Daena dives in. Ari is taken back by her power and grace in the water.

EXT. UNDER WATER – FOLLOW DAENA

She swims powerfully. Pulls apart a curtain of weeds. REVEALING: THE POD. Daena is amazed. She runs her hand along the surface.

PUSH EXTREME CLOSE: the emblem of the *Oberon* on the pod. The letters "USAF." INTO FRAME — Leo swims out of the pod carrying a METALLIC BOX. They turn to swim back.

FILLING FRAME — the bodies of the two soldier apes Thade has murdered.

Daena *reacts* — Leo pulls her away.

EXT. BOG

Leo and Daena swim quickly back to shore. Leo looks at Krull.

LEO
You guys don't go near water?

Leo sets the EMERGENCY BOX (with an *OBERON* LOGO) on the ground.

LEO (cont'd)
How come there's two monkeys down there?

They all *react* —

KRULL
Someone else knows about you.

CLOSER: Leo urgently unpacks the box.

Removes a LAPTOP-SIZED DEVICE. While Leo works to set it up, Birn rummages through the box.

Out come: Compass, flare, MRE's (field rations), thermal blanket, cord, medical kit. Birn passes around the supplies; the others examine them, not sure what they're for. Gunnar tears open the field rations. The contents spill to the ground.

Leo's box suddenly SQUAWKS to life. The humans jump back.

ARI
What is it?

LEO
It's called a Messenger ... it keeps an open frequency with my ship so I can talk to them.

ARI
It can talk?

LEO
With radio waves.
(off their confused look)
Invisible energy that floats all around us.

KRULL
This is sorcery.

LEO
Not sorcery, science ... I just have to monkey with it a little.

Ari and Krull *react.*

A LOUD PIERCING TONE startles them all. Ari and Krull cover their ears. Leo is electrified.

LEO (cont'd)
Contact.

Birn creeps forward to peek at the machine. ON THE MESSENGER SCREEN: a digital SWEEP shows Leo's position and the position of the responding beacon. Leo's face lights up brightly.

LEO (cont'd)
Jesus. They're already here.

CLOSE ON ARI — amazed.

DAENA
You'd better warn them about the apes.

LEO
Better warn the apes about *them.
We're* in control now. *We're* the 800-pound gorilla.

ARI
It's time you told us the truth ... Who are you?

PUSH IN CLOSE on Leo as he turns to them —

LEO
I'm Captain Leo Davidson, of the United States *Oberon*. I come from a galaxy called the Milky Way. A planet in our star system called Earth.

BIRN
Is it far?

LEO
Past any star you can see at night.

An impossible concept. CLOSE ON ARI: Her look reveals how much Leo has taken hold of her imagination.

TIVAL
Your apes permit you to fly?

LEO
Our apes live in zoos ... They do what we tell them ...

Leo quickly closes up the Messenger.

LEO (cont'd)
I'd call this hostile territory. So I've got exactly 36 hours to rendezvous with them ... And then my ass is out of this nightmare.

GUNNAR
What happens to us? Where do we go?

EXT. BOG — CONTINUOUS

ANGLE — dropping out of the trees

LIMBO slams down on Gunnar and holds him tight.

LIMBO
You're going nowhere. This one still belongs to me.

Gunnar struggles but Limbo slaps him once — and stuns him. Limbo shackles his legs.

ARI
This is an outrage ... *stop.*

LIMBO (*growls* at her)
You I've had enough of.

WIDEN

Birn breaks for the forest. He's pulled off the ground. TILT UP: Two of Limbo's handlers explode from bushes.

CLOSE ON LEO

He quietly reaches into the emergency box. Takes out a SIDEARM and setting his finger on the trigger makes a rapid adjustment to the handle.

Birn fights fiercely as Limbo tries to shackle him.

LIMBO (cont'd)
Hold still. I'm not going to hurt you. I wouldn't hurt my own property ...

Birn punches him sharply in the face. Limbo *growls* and backhands him hard.

LIMBO (cont'd)
For you I'll make an exception.

He's about to hit Birn again — PAN SLIGHTLY RIGHT — as the tree branch next to Limbo suddenly explodes. Wood splinters. The sound echoes through the forest. It's never been heard before by any of them. Birn stares wide-eyed at Leo.

LEO (re: gun)
You saw what it did to the tree.

Limbo's men are as loyal as he is honest; they disappear into the trees. Limbo freezes. Gives a meek smile. Quickly helps Birn to his feet.

LIMBO
No harm done.
(to Birn)
You're not hurt. You're young ...
(smiles at Leo)
... these kids bounce right back.

LEO (as if commanding a dog)
Play dead.

Limbo falls to his knees, puts his hands up.

DAENA
Kill him!

Gunnar kicks Limbo.

GUNNAR
Slave trader.

But Ari steps in the way.

ARI
If you kill him, you'll only lower yourself to his level.

LIMBO
Exactly. She's extremely smart. You know, I've heard her talking ... about apes and humans ... (fumbling)
Separate but equal, to each his own ... something like that, right? Whatever it is, I agree with it completely.

Limbo approaches Leo with his hands up (the way we saw him disarm Leo in the quadrangle).

LIMBO (cont'd)
Can't we all just get along?

Leo fires at the ground just before Limbo makes a move to grab the gun with his foot.

LEO
Find a new trick.
(re: Gunnar's shackles)
Take them off ...

Limbo frees Gunnar from the heavy shackles.

LIMBO
Well, I'm probably just in the way now. So I'll get going ...

He tries to back away.

DAENA
He'll lead them to us.

LEO
Then we'll make him our guest.

Leo throws the shackles to Birn. Birn locks Limbo's wrists.

LIMBO
Ow! These things hurt.

INTO FRAME from above Leo — KRULL flips down and grabs the gun from Leo. Jumps to the ground.

LEO
What the hell are you doing?

KRULL
You can turn this on me. I can't allow it.

Before Leo can stop Krull, he uses his massive strength to smash the gun against a rock. Ari scolds Leo.

ARI
Who would invent such a horrible device?

LEO (screams)
That "device" was going to keep me alive.

ARI
We're better off without it.

DAENA
There's no "we" here.

ARI
Must you be so difficult?

DAENA
Why don't I act more like a slave?

ARI
That's not what I meant.

As they argue —

LEO
Shut up ... That goes for all species.

Ari and Daena separate, then —

DAENA
You can't trust them.

LEO
Know who I trust? Myself.

Leo picks up the Messenger and hurries off.

NEW ANGLE — Ape soldiers move through the city.

FIND THADE — walking with SANDAR, Ari's father.

SANDAR
If I ever thought that those humans were capable of kidnapping my daughter ...

Sandar's voice breaks.

THADE
Don't blame yourself, Senator. Your family above all tried to be compassionate to the humans ... and look how they repaid you.

Sandar seems suddenly frail and weak.

SANDAR
Can you find my daughter?

THADE
If you untie my hands.

Sandar is caught off guard.

SANDAR
What do you want?

Thade stops — turns to him boldly.

THADE
Declare martial law. Give me the absolute power to rid our planet of humans once and for all.

When Sandar hesitates —

THADE (cont'd)
Now is not the time to be timid and indecisive ...
(steps closer)
... I am the only one who can bring your daughter back to you ... alive.

Sandar looks at him — nods, then leaves quickly.

ANGLE

Attar comes up to Thade.

ATTAR
They're not within the city walls.

THADE
We underestimate this human.

Thade considers, then —

THADE (cont'd)
I will hunt him down myself.

He mounts his horse.

ANGLE

An OLD APE SERVANT in dark robes rides up.

OLD APE
Your father has sent me to find you. You must come quickly.

Thade is shaken by the news. He gives orders to Attar.

THADE
Alert our outposts. Make sure the human does not pass.

ATTAR
I understand, sir.

Thade looks at Attar.

THADE
Except for my father, you're the one I depend on most. We are not just soldiers ... we're friends. I'm depending on you.

INT. THADE'S FATHER'S HOUSE – NIGHT

A pitch-dark room. Windows shrouded. A single candle BURNS by a wooden bed. Silence broken only by the rasp of heavy breathing.

CLOSER: IN THE BED

An extremely frail, old APE, fur completely gray. So insubstantial he seems to have no corporeality.

INTO THE LIGHT: THADE

startled by the pitiful shell of his father. We read great pain in Thade's face. He reaches out and touches the old ape.

THADE
Father ...

The old ape opens his eyes — cataracts distort their color. He smiles when he recognizes his son.

FATHER
I don't have much time ... Tell me about this human who troubles you.

THADE
He'll be captured soon ... and little trouble.

FATHER
You're not telling me everything ...

You believe he's not born of this world.

CLOSE ON THADE: he *reacts* — surprised.

FATHER (cont'd)
Has he come alone?

THADE
Yes.

FATHER
More will come looking for him.

THADE
How can you possibly know?

FATHER
I have something to tell you before I die. Something my father told me ... and his father told him ... back across our bloodline to Semos.

PUSH IN CLOSE as Thade leans his ear to his father's lips.

FATHER (cont'd)
In the time before time ... we were the slaves and the humans were our masters.

THADE
Impossible.

Thade's Father holds out his skeletal hand and points across the room. On a table sits a sealed URN.

FATHER
Break it.

Thade hurries across the room. Smashes the urn to the floor.

INSERT: ON THE FLOOR

In the clay pieces Thade finds what looks like an ancient metal artifact. A GUN. Thade holds it up, confused.

FATHER (cont'd)
What you hold in your hand is proof of their power. Their power of invention. Their power of technology. Against which our strength means nothing.

Thade looks at the gun, holds it, studies it.

FATHER (cont'd)
It has the force of a thousand spears.

Greatly agitated, Thade's Father grimaces in pain; he fights to stay lucid.

FATHER (cont'd)
I warn you ... their ingenuity goes hand in hand with their cruelty. No creature is as devious or violent ... Find this human quickly ... do not let him reach Calima.

THADE
The ancient ruins? There's nothing there but some old cave paintings.

FATHER
Calima holds the secret of our true beginning.

The old ape groans in great pain.

THADE
I will stop him, Father.

FATHER
This human has already infected the others with his ideas.
(with his last breath)
Damn them all to Hell ...

His hand drops away. His eyes roll back. Thade's eyes well with tears. He closes his father's eyes — and blows out the candle.

EXT. MOUNTAIN SLOPES – DAY

Rough and steep. Leo and the other humans struggle towards the top.

EXT. MOUNTAIN SLOPES – CONTINUOUS

Leo stops to catch his breath. Tival and Krull immediately tend to Ari again. This time Ari bounds right to Leo and hands him the water. Leo reacts — unsettled by her intimate manner with him. Leo takes a sip. Returns it to her.

NEW ANGLE: Daena is watching them. Ari holds out the canteen to her. Daena brushes it aside. Moves on.

WIDEN (MOVING) — as Leo and Ari walk.

Ari is excited, full of energy.

ARI
I have so many questions I want to ask.

LEO
Get in line.

ARI
What are these "zoos" you speak of? ... This word is unfamiliar.

LEO
Zoos are where you'll find our last few apes.

Ari and Krull *react.*

KRULL
What happened to the rest of them?

LEO
Gone. After we cut down their forests. The ones that survived we lock in cages for our amusement ... or use in scientific experiments.

ARI (shocked and angry)
How horrible.

LEO
We do worse to our own kind.

ARI
I don't understand ... you seem to possess such great intelligence.

LEO
Yeah, we're pretty smart ... and the smarter we get the more dangerous our world becomes.

Ari looks at Leo. No matter what he says she'll find a way to use it as a connection.

ARI
You're sensitive, I knew it. It is an uncommon quality in a male.

KRULL
Why don't your apes object to the way you treat them?

LEO
Our apes can't talk.

ARI
Maybe they choose not to, given the way you treat them.

Limbo snorts — he doesn't believe a word.

LIMBO
Apes in cages. Right.

DAENA
Sounds like paradise to me.

EXT. MOUNTAIN SLOPES – CONTINUOUS

WIDEN

BIRN is watching Leo. Leo smiles at him. Birn is embarrassed — scoots ahead. The hill becomes very steep now. Birn looks for something to grab onto.

CLOSE ON BIRN'S HAND — he latches onto an APE FOOT.

PAN UP to see a monstrous ape — arms spread wide — canines exposed. Birn *screams* and tumbles backward. FOLLOW BIRN caroming down the hill.

INTO FRAME — SOMEONE catches him. Birn looks up to see Leo.

LEO
They're not real.

REVEAL: APE EFFIGIES. Exaggerated in size, set in fearsome poses, hanging from high poles. A long line along the crest of the hill.

Daena steps beside Leo.

DAENA
The apes put them where they don't want us to go. Crossing means certain death.

LEO
What's so important on the other side of this hill?

KRULL
It leads to the ancient ruins at Calima.

LEO
Calima?

ARI
Our holy writings say Creation

began at Calima ... where the Almighty breathed life into Semos, the First Ape, in the time before time ...

KRULL
... and where it is said Semos will return to us one day.

ARI
Of course, most educated apes consider such religious notions as fairytales, metaphors we use to explain our origins. I doubt there ever really was a Semos.

DAENA
His friends aren't fairytales. They're real.

Leo continues across the line of EFFIGIES. Krull shoves Limbo ahead.

LIMBO
Doesn't he ever stop?

STAY ON HUMANS: afraid to cross the line. Birn suddenly springs forward. TILT UP at the effigy as Birn chases past it to fall behind Leo. Daena sees it — and runs after them with the others.

EXT. TOP OF THE HILL — EVENING

Leo finally reaches the crest. Below is a narrow MEADOW in a valley between two MOUNTAINS. A dozen patterned TENTS form a camp by a river. APES guard the pass.

Leo and the others hide in the ROCKS.

POV — A SMALL HERD OF HORSES trapped in a natural rock pen between Leo and the Ape Camp.

DAENA (re: horses)
Monsters.

LEO (reacts)
What are you talking about?

GUNNAR
I've heard the apes feed them human flesh.

TIVAL
I've heard they're possessed by the spirits of great ape generals.

LEO
They're just horses. They'll do whatever you tell them to do.

GUNNAR
We should to cross the river another way ... over the mountains.

LEO
I've got no time for that. We'll go through them.

Leo slips back down the hill. Ari and Krull exchange a look. Limbo calls after him.

LIMBO
Where should we bury your remains?

EXT. APE ENCAMPMENT — NIGHT

Brightly colored tents billow in the wind off the river.

By a campfire — a group of ape soldiers are gambling. ONE APE throws down a large PLAYING CARD.

INSERT PLAYING CARD: The figures are apes in ancient costumes

FIRST APE SOLDIER
Semos smiles on me. I win again.

He reaches for the pot. A SECOND APE SOLDIER stops his arm.

SECOND APE SOLDIER
You win too often. What have you hidden up your sleeve?

It immediately gets tense. The FIRST SOLDIER pulls back the sleeves of his uniform. One hand, the other hand. Grins — nothing there. Reaches for the pot again. He's stopped again.

SECOND APE SOLDIER (cont'd)
All of them ...

He forces back one pant leg. Nothing in that foot. Tries the other. PUNCH IN CLOSE: The first ape holds a card with his foot.

SECOND APE SOLDIER (cont'd)
Cheater!

He knocks the soldier back. In a second they start to fight. A loud *growl* makes them stop. They turn to see —

ATTAR ON HORSEBACK, having just come into camp. He has clearly covered a great distance. He rides right up to them and kicks over the cards. The soldiers jump to their feet.

ATTAR (OS)
Who is in charge here?

ANGLE: Rushing out of a TENT: the APE COMMANDER, quickly buttoning his uniform.

APE COMMANDER
I am, sir. ... They didn't tell me you were coming.

ATTAR (cuts him off)
This camp is a disgrace.

The Commander is terrified. Attar dismounts.

ATTAR (cont'd)
Some humans have escaped.

APE COMMANDER
If they come this way we'll crush them.

ATTAR
These humans are different. They travel with apes.

The Ape Commander hesitates, then laughs —

ATTAR (cont'd)
You find this amusing?

APE COMMANDER (stops)
No, sir.

Attar looks around at the mountains.

ATTAR
I'm assuming command. I will personally make sure this camp is prepared.

EXT. HORSE PEN — NIGHT

Leo holds a DUN-COLORED

STALLION. They watch him grab a fistful of mane and hop on. The humans are all amazed. Leo wheels the horse round.

LEO
Who's next?

The others hang back. Too afraid to join him.

LEO (cont'd)
Then I guess we're saying goodbye here.

Ari takes a hesitant step forward.

DAENA
You can't go, you're afraid of water.

ARI
You can't go, you're afraid of horses.

Leo rides between them.

LEO (to Daena)
You want to ride? Grab a fistful of mane and hold on.
(to Ari)
You want to cross the river? Horses are great swimmers. They'll carry you across ...

KRULL appears out of the darkness.

KRULL
You're assuming the soldiers won't tear you to pieces ... I've just seen Thade's greatest warrior ride into the camp.

LEO
Sounds like he scares you.

KRULL
He does. I trained him myself.

LIMBO
Well, good luck, have a pleasant ride. Obviously, I can't go ... so if you don't mind ...

He holds out his shackles. Leo surprises everyone by unlocking them.

DAENA
You're letting him go?

The shackles fall — Limbo sighs, rubs his wrists.

LEO
No. He'll ride with us.

LIMBO
There is no way ...

ARI (over)
And if you try to get away, I will tell Thade we bribed you to help us.

LIMBO
I'll deny it.

KRULL
A very large bribe.

Ari and Krull grin at him. Limbo explodes.

LIMBO
The whole thing's suicide. Ride through an army encampment? Only a human would think this could work.

LEO
Attitude is the first human freedom.

Leo reaches into the Messenger box, takes out the FLARE GUN.

EXT. APE ENCAMPMENT – NIGHT

CLOSE ON ATTAR — inside a tent, kneeling on a small woven tapestry. Eyes closed. Candles illuminate a small ICON of SEMOS emerging out of PARTING CLOUDS. Attar waves his hands over the smoke. Bows his head.

A LOUD WHOOSH — and the tent is bathed in LIGHT. Attar OPENS his eyes.

EXT. TENT – AROUND THE CAMP

Attar rushes out to see the soldiers staring at the sky.

IN THE SKY — a blinding light; actually, an army FLARE, raining down on them. CLOSE ON ATTAR — he cocks an ear — listening intently.

OVER HIS SHOULDER: stampeding into view — HORSES

CLOSER — Leo leads the group. Birn and Daena right behind. Tival, Gunnar, then Krull and Ari. Finally, Limbo — holding on for dear life.

WIDEN

Leo has let the extra horses run with them. The apes dive out of the way as the horses stampede through them. Tents are pulled down. Equipment crushed. The sheer arrogance of Leo's maneuver leaves Attar stunned.

CLOSE ON LIMBO as he rides, holding on tightly. He kicks the horse so it veers away toward the ape soldiers.

LIMBO
Help, help. Don't hurt me. I'm on your side.

But to Limbo's surprise the ape soldiers answer with a barrage of fireballs. One nicks Limbo's arm. Limbo is stunned. An ape soldier charges Limbo with a spear. Limbo can't get his horse to move.

INTO FRAME — Leo whacks Limbo's horse. It carries Limbo to the river. Leo leans down to grab a burning log and ignites one of the ape tents. The fire spreads as if burning dry grass. Whipped by the wind. One ape runs out of a tent with his fur on fire.

Leo charges for the river.

EXT. THE RIVER – NIGHT (CONTINUOUS)

Deep and wide. PAN UP TO — the horses reflected in the water.

LEO
Drive them across!

Daena feels the power of her horse as it splashes into the water. Birn has a big smile on his face as his horse lunges through the river. Tival grips the mane tightly as his horse goes in. Finally, Krull's horse carries him in.

EXT. APE ENCAMPMENT — CONTINUOUS

FIND ARI — lagging far behind. Her eyes wide with terror. Using all her will to fight the panic building up inside.

ATTAR — sees Ari.

WIDEN

Before Ari reaches the river, Attar hurls his *bola* — it wraps around the horse's front feet and brings it down. Ari flies off, rolling across the ground.

LEO sees Ari fall. He turns his horse and races for her.

EXT. THE RIVER — CONTINUOUS

Daena, Birn, Gunnar, and Tival emerge on the opposite bank. Krull appears behind them. He falls from the horse. Looks for Ari. Runs back to the water's edge.

POV — on the other side, Krull can see Ari head for the rocks. She starts to climb. The apes are moving out of camp toward her. Krull is enraged he can't protect her. Lets out a fierce *roar*.

CLOSE ON ATTAR — he hears Krull. They lock eyes across the river. It makes Attar hesitate for just one moment.

FIND LEO — He rides for the rocks and leaps from his horse. Scrambles up to Ari. Grabs her hand.

LEO
You have to swim.

Ari can't bring herself to enter the river. Her instinctual aversion is just too strong. Her eyes are wide with terror.

LEO'S POV: Rushing out of the night, all he can see is Attar's eyes.

ARI
I can't.

LEO
I won't let go of you.

Attar arrives just as Ari and Leo leap off the rocks into the river and disappear beneath the dark water.

The apes hurl fireballs after them, but they only *hiss* and turn to steam in the river.

EXT. ACROSS THE RIVER — NIGHT

Krull is still at the water's edge when Ari's horse emerges riderless. Krull is shaken to the core.

Finally, Limbo rides up. Falls to the ground soggy and miserable. Still reeling. He looks at the small burn on his fur. *Whimpers* as he licks it.

Gunnar comes up with the shackles.

LIMBO
No, no, wait, there's no need now.

GUNNAR
Says who?

Limbo gestures angrily across the water.

LIMBO
Says them. They tried to kill me ...
(touches his wound again)
... like I was nothing but a miserable ...

DAENA
Human?

GUNNAR
He's a liar and a coward.

PUSH IN ECU on Limbo — he's too smart not to understand what this all means. His usual bravado melts away.

LIMBO (softly)
Please, I've nowhere else to go.

Tival steps in front of Gunnar, helps Limbo to his feet.

TIVAL
Then you belong with us.

GUNNAR
We're the only ones who made it. I say we should to stick to our own kind.

Daena isn't sure what to do. She gives way to her doubts. Looks at Krull.

DAENA
It's no use. Nothing will ever change.

Birn suddenly sprints toward the water. They all turn —

EXT. ACROSS THE RIVER — CONTINUOUS

ANGLE — staggering out of the river

Leo carries Ari on his back. Ari's claws dig tightly into his shoulder. It is a potent vision that contradicts the core reality of their planet — and their races. HOLD ON Daena's reaction as the others rush down to help them. Leo sets Ari on the ground.

Krull takes Ari's hand. She knows how worried he was about her. She strokes his fur, comforting him.

ANGLE

Daena pushes through to Leo. Looks at his shoulders. Ari's claws have left deep cuts.

DAENA
She hurt you.

Daena slaps a clump of wet leaves on the wounds.

LEO
She was holding on pretty tight.

She begins to rub his shoulders. Slowly, deeply.

DAENA
I know. I've seen the way she looks at you.

LEO (reacting)
She's a chimpanzee.

DAENA
A female chimpanzee.

Leo is freaked out by the conversation. Daena rubs harder.

LEO
Ow ...

DAENA
These are Goma leaves.

LEO
And they're supposed to help?

Now she's really working the shoulder.

DAENA
First your body will tingle, then you'll feel very dizzy ...

Leo looks at her, confused.

DAENA (cont'd)
... and if you don't start growing fur everywhere ... you'll be healed.

CLOSE ON LEO — as he realizes she's been teasing him. Daena laughs, and the other humans join in. Leo knows the joke's on him. Leo and Daena look at each other. She has a wickedly defiant look on her face.

PAN ACROSS TO ARI — who *reacts* to their intimacy. She gets up quickly. Bounds across to them.

ARI
The apes will head downriver til they find a crossing. We should keep moving.

Leo stands. Daena locks eyes with Ari.

DAENA
You've recovered quickly.

Tival signals Leo; points to the cliffs.

EXT. CLIFFS — PUNCH INTO POV — IN THE CLIFFS

TWO HUMAN MALES stare down at them from the shadows. Their faces have distinct tribal markings (we'll see them again). As soon as they're spotted, they disappear.

EXT. CITY OF THE APES — ARMY HEADQUARTERS — DAY

THE TROOPS are massed in the city square, waiting. Attar stands at the entrance to the headquarters. Thade enters from inside. They walk and talk.

THADE
Where is he?

Attar is ashamed to look at Thade.

ATTAR
They crossed the river.

Thade's voice is quiet, intense.

THADE
You didn't stop them?

ATTAR
They were carried by horses.

Attar can hardly bear the silence while Thade glares at him. It seems an eternity — until Thade finally speaks, his anger now building.

THADE
Horses?

ATTAR
Yes, sir. *Our* horses.

We see Thade's essential ape nature take over. He moves quickly, leaping up the walls, pulling down tapestries, swinging up to the overhead chandelier. He draws his sword and with one forceful move cuts down the chandelier. It crashes to the ground, carrying Thade down with it, and bursts into flames.

Thade moves through the flames and mounts his horse. He turns toward Attar, takes a breath, calms himself. Thade looks into Attar's eyes. His rage melts as quickly as it came on.

THADE
Forgive me? I'm not angry at you ... My father has been taken from me.

He embraces Attar emotionally. Attar consoles him.

ATTAR
He was a great leader ... Your family are direct descendents of Semos. Now it is time for you to lead.

Thade looks at Attar — steadfast, loyal as always, then composes himself.

THADE
Form the divisions.

WIDEN

Attar hurries to the troops. Turns to his lieutenants.

ATTAR
Form the divisions. Full battle ready. Sound the call to march ...

EXT. CITY OF THE APES

QUICK SHOTS: APE BUGLERS start the clarion call. DRUMMERS beat a marching rhythm. Troops fall into line.

WIDE SHOT: EXT. CITY OF THE APES — GATE

Thade rides in front of his army as it marches to war.

EXT. PLAINS — ON THE WAY TO CALIMA — NIGHT

CAMPFIRE

Krull walks off by himself and assumes a "guard" position. Ari and Leo watch him.

ARI
He'll stand like that all night.

LEO
No question, he's army. I know the type.

ARI
Maybe we're more alike than you think.

Leo *reacts*. Ari looks up at the stars.

ARI (cont'd)
I'd like to see your world.

LEO
No, you wouldn't. They'd prod you and poke you and throw you in a cage, too.

ARI
You'd protect me.

She gently reaches over and touches his arm. Waits for his reply.

LEO
You'd never be able to go home again.

ARI
I can't go home now.

LEO
I can't take you with me ... You're right. We are alike. It's just as dangerous for you on my world as it is for me here.

There is heartbreak in Ari's voice.

ARI
I think after tomorrow, when you find your friends ... I'll never see you again.

LEO
I never promised anyone anything.

Ari looks over at Tival, Birn, and Gunnar.

ARI
That's not what they think ... they think you're going to save them.

PAN ACROSS — Daena is watching them as she sits with the other humans grabbing food, shoving it to their mouths as quickly as they can. Daena watches Ari break her food into small pieces; it seems refined, elegant.

Daena looks down at her hand.

Drops her food. Breaks off one small bit. Mimics Ari.

TIVAL (sitting INTO FRAME)
It's not the way she eats, it's the way she thinks that pleases him.

Daena looks at him, embarrassed, then — runs off.

EXT. PLAINS — FOLLOW DAENA

Til she's by herself. She stops at a small trail of water dribbling down a rock face. Looks around nervously. CLOSER — Daena takes a small soft piece of cloth. Touches the water. Disrobes quickly. Starts to wash herself.

EXT. CALIMA — DAWN

Leo leads the others over a small ridge.

POV — Across the plain, through the haze, he can just make out the ruins.

KRULL
Calima.

Leo dismounts. PUSH IN CLOSE: as Leo opens the MESSENGER again. The others gather around.

INSERT: MESSENGER SCREEN. The BEACON sounds loudly, bouncing off the walls, sweeping with precision.

EXT. CALIMA — THE PLAINS

Leo jumps up — leaps onto the horse and streaks for the source of the signal. The others chase behind.

Leo moves faster and faster. The beacon leading him on. Excited, expecting the crew to be right there.

EXT. CALIMA RUINS

TILT UP INTO POV as Leo gets his first clean look at Calima. Eerie, silent. Leo holds up the beacon — it sounds louder than ever.

The others have followed. They wait for him to say something. Leo can't

hide what he's thinking; they see it on his face.

GUNNAR (realizing)
They're not here.

The notion leaves them unable to speak. Gunnar explodes.

GUNNAR (cont'd)
They were never here.

Daena's voice betrays her fear —

DAENA
But ... you said they'd come for you.

Ari, Krull, and Limbo are watching. Limbo sniffs —

LIMBO
I know this smell ... right, it's a catastrophe.

Leo is reeling. He dashes down a STONE PASSAGEWAY.

EXT. CALIMA – CAVE ENTRANCE – DOWN A STONE PATH

Leo looks around. The beeping of the Messenger becomes louder.

INT. CALIMA CAVE

We move with Leo's POV as he moves deeper and deeper inside. We can hear Leo breathing hard. The cave slopes downward sharply.

At first it just seems like nothing more than a rock cave. His foot kicks something hard in the ground.

SOMETHING WHITE in the dirt

Leo kneels and digs into the ground. Reaches in. Leo rises with a round

clump of dirt. He breaks it clear. It's a HUMAN SKULL. Leo drops it. Looks around: HUMAN BONES are scattered along the cave.

PUNCH IN CLOSE ON LEO

He looks at the walls again. *He's been here before.*

Leo picks up a rock — starts to scrape at the CAVE WALL. Works frantically. Soil crumbles to the ground. Leo hits something METALLIC. Clears it away with his hands.

ON THE WALL: Reveal the *Oberon* icon that we saw in the corridor on the wall of the station.

CIRCLE LEO — fighting this impossible revelation.

LEO
No, no ...

ECU: Leo holds up his brand against the icon. It's a clipped section of the *Oberon*'s emblem. Leo looks at the contours and shapes of the cavern. It can't be. But everything matches the way he remembers it.

This is the Oberon.

FOLLOW LEO

He dashes down what looks like a stone tunnel. Leo stops in one "cave" — chips at the rock revealing the animal cages of the *Oberon*. Rusted and coated with limestone. Leo walks up to the warning sign we saw in the beginning:

CAUTION: LIVE ANIMALS — but all that remains of the original letters is: CA   LI   MA ... CALIMA

KEEP MOVING with Leo to where the bridge security door should be. He chips dust from the HAND ID SYSTEM.

ECU: Leo reaches one trembling hand out. Nothing. Beat — then a *hum* starts from deep inside the cave. A faint light glows. Then the glass wall begins to slide open. Dust spills into the air.

Leo staggers into the BRIDGE ROOM.

INT. CALIMA CAVE/*OBERON* BRIDGE

Daena and Ari move warily toward the source of the LIGHT.

POV: Leo stands in the middle of the great space. Deep in thought. Trying to regain hold of his emotions.

Daena steps closer.

DAENA
What is it?

Leo can barely bring himself to say the words.

LEO
It's ... *my ship.*

ARI
But ... these ruins are thousands of years old.

LEO
I was here ... just a few days ago.

Leo moves over to the CONTROL PANEL, furiously pulls away soil and dust. Ari and Daena watch as Leo lights up the board. Now Leo can read the DIGITAL DATE as it flashes by in milliseconds:

5021.946

Leo begins to work the board. The entire BRIDGE lights up in stages.

Daena and Ari look around. It is as profoundly incredible to them as landing on the planet was to Leo.

Leo pushes the red TRACKING LEVER we saw him use in the first scene. CLOSE ON the ship's MES-SENGER BEACON — Leo watches it pulse and sweep the screen.

LEO (cont'd)
This is what my Messenger was picking up. The *Oberon*.

Leo forces open another CONTROL BOX. Begins punching numbers.

ARI
What are you doing?

LEO
Accessing the database. Every ship keeps a visual log ...

DAENA
I don't understand.

LEO
A way for them to tell their own story.

ARI
Will it work?

LEO
This ship has a nuclear power source with a half life of forever.

INT. CALIMA CAVE/*OBERON* BRIDGE

Leo sweeps away dust from the giant digital screen above them. LIGHT floods out — blinding them all for a moment.

Leo starts scrolling through a time-coded visual log.

The digital date begins to roll backward.

ON THE SCREEN: A blur of images, jumpy, ripped by binary static. Leo suddenly sees Vasich. His face burned and scarred. His voice tremulous.

VASICH (on screen)
... we were searching for a pilot lost in an electromagnetic storm ... When we got close, our guidance systems went down ...

LEO
They couldn't find me ... because I was punched forward through time.

VASICH (on screen)
... we've received no communi-cations since we crash-landed. This planet is uncharted and uninhabited ... We're trying to make the best of it ... the apes we brought along have been helpful. They're stronger and smarter than we ever imagined ...

The screen disappears in static. Leo continues to scroll, looking for undamaged bits of log.

INT. CALIMA CAVE/*OBERON* BRIDGE

ON DIGITAL SCREEN: More static. Leo scrolls through again. He can't read any of the images.

INT. CALIMA CAVE/*OBERON* BRIDGE – CONTINUOUS – SUDDENLY ON THE SCREEN

Leo finds ALEXANDER, with long silver hair. Maybe sixty years old. A weary, distressed glaze to her eyes. We HEAR strange NOISES O.S. The sound of a door being battered as if under siege.

ALEXANDER
... the others have fled with the children to the mountains ... The apes are out of control. One male named Semos, who I raised myself, has taken over the pack. He's extremely brutal.
(voice breaks)
We have some weapons but ... I don't know how much longer we'll last.

Alexander keeps looking back over her shoulder.

ALEXANDER (cont'd)
... Maybe I saw the truth when they were young and wouldn't admit it. We taught them too well. They were apt pupils ...

In one quick blur we see FOUR LARGE APES sweep across the screen — ONE APE (SEMOS) looks right at the camera. Then *growls* in a rage and reaches out at camera. The screen turns to pure static.

Leo finally reaches out and changes controls.

ON THE SCREEN: the names of the crew. Leo scrolls through them all until he stops on his own name:

CAPTAIN LEO DAVIDSON: MISSING IN ACTION

PUNCH IN CLOSE ON LEO — staring at his name — stunned, his eyes glisten. INTO FRAME — ARI kneels by him, tries to console him.

LEO
The crash, their deaths ... they're all dead because they were looking for me.

ARI
But we're all alive because of you.

Leo fumbles with some of the gauges.

LEO
There's a little power left in one of the fuel rods.

DAENA
You're trying to find a way to leave us.

CLOSE ON LEO — looks around the ship longingly.

LEO
I've been away from home a thousand years.

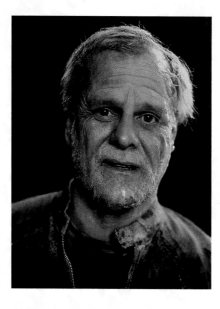

EXT. CALIMA — THE RUINS

Leo, Ari, and Daena emerge into the light. The others follow close behind. Leo can see DARK SHAPES emerge out of the haze. Surrounding the ruins.

CLOSER — A large group of HUMANS waits at the ruins. They carry belongings and homemade weapons. Led by the TWO HUMANS with distinctive tribal markings we saw at the river crossing. Scores of others join them.

LEO
Who the hell are they?

TIVAL
Your story is spreading through the villages ... They all want to see this human who defies the apes.

LEO
Send them back.

DAENA
Back where? They've left their homes to be with you.

EXT. CALIMA RUINS — FOLLOW LEO THROUGH THE CROWD

As soon as the humans see Leo, a great CHEER spreads among them like wildfire. They crowd around him. Limbo wedges himself next to Leo.

LIMBO
See if you can talk your space friends into taking me ... 'cause whichever way this goes, I'm out of business.

Leo pushes away forward.

EXT. CALIMA RUINS — CONTINUE WITH LEO THROUGH THE HUMANS

Families, loners, the old, and the young. Some touch his hand. The humans glare at Ari, some curious, most hostile.

OUT OF THE CROWD: A HUMAN FIGURE confronts Ari. It's BON — Ari's old servant. They embrace with tears. The Little Human Girl that Bon saved hides behind Bon, shy and wary. But Ari kneels and smiles at her. Slowly, the Little Girl lets Ari take her into her arms. The Little Girl finally smiles back at Ari.

EXT. CALIMA CLIFF'S EDGE – SUNSET – SECOND NIGHT

As sunset turns the sky to fire, Leo stands on the cliff — looking out over the Plain of Calima. His face a study in concern.

EXT. CALIMA PLAINS – NIGHT

Vast and empty. Birn on horseback. Watching. POV: From behind a distant hill he sees a strange glow. Kicks his horse. Rides quickly to the crest.

WIDEN TO POV

In the far distance he can see a LINE OF TORCHES snaking all the way to the horizon.

REVEAL Thade's army — on the move, led by DRUMMERS beating out a rhythm. An endless stream of Apes of all kinds — in full battle gear — storm ACROSS FRAME. Moving with incredible speed.

Attar leads his division past Thade, mounted on an elaborately caparisoned horse.

BACK TO BIRN — he spins his horse and races away.

EXT. CALIMA RUINS – NIGHT

Suddenly Birn comes galloping in on his horse. Jumps off. Runs up to Leo.

> **BIRN**
> I saw them.

> **KRULL**
> How many?

> **BIRN**
> As far as I could see.

Krull *reacts* —

> **KRULL**
> Thade has brought all his legions.

That means the Senate has capitulated. He answers to no one now.

Leo turns to Daena.

> **LEO**
> Get your people away from here. They can go to the mountains, hide ... while there's still a chance.

> **DAENA**
> They won't listen to me.

Leo thinks about it, then —

> **LEO**
> OK, if they came here to follow me, I'll let them follow.

EXT. CALIMA RUINS – WIDEN – NIGHT

The humans wait for Leo to talk to them. He mounts his horse.

> **LEO**
> This is a fight we can't win ... break up and scatter. I'll draw them off. I'm the one they want ... Let's go ...

He spins his horse and starts to ride. STAY WITH LEO as he moves out.

Then Leo stops, turns around —

WIDEN TO POV: The humans have not moved. They remain silently by the rocks.

Leo gallops back to Daena. Dismounts.

> **LEO** (cont'd)
> They don't understand. It's over. Finished. There's no help coming.

She looks deeply at him. Touches her hand to his face.

> **DAENA**
> You came ...

She leans in and kisses him.

WIDE SHOT: EXT. CALIMA – THADE'S APE ENCAMPMENT – NIGHT

An eerie silence pervades the APE CAMP. A thousand campfires seem to make the sky glow.

In the shadows, a LARGE FIGURE moves furtively past the tents.

EXT. CALIMA – THADE'S APE ENCAMPMENT –
CLOSE ON ATTAR

in a dark mood. At the edge of the
camp. Staring out across the plains to
Calima. He hears something.
Footsteps. INTO FRAME — a figure.

ATTAR
Stop! ...

Attar's senses come alive. Something
jolts him.

ATTAR (cont'd)
Come closer and identify yourself!

The FIGURE hesitates. Then moves
toward them. It's KRULL.

Attar is caught by surprise seeing his
teacher. For a second he even seems
defensive. Then —

ATTAR (cont'd)
You dare show your face here?

KRULL
It was not my decision ...

Krull steps aside. Stepping from
behind is ARI.

ARI
I wish to speak to Thade.

ATTAR
Impossible. You have betrayed
your race.

KRULL
And you have betrayed everything
that I taught you.

ATTAR
I could have you killed on the spot.

KRULL (a low *growl*, then)
You could try.

Ari steps between them. Tries to
reason with Attar.

ARI
Don't you ever think we apes have
lost our way? Don't you ever have
doubts?

She can see Attar is affected by
her words.

INT. THADE'S TENT – NIGHT

Ari stands with her head down.

THADE
Why have you come?

ARI
To be with you. Isn't it what you want?

QUICK CUT: Outside the tent, Krull and Attar stand — eyeing each other.

BACK INSIDE THE TENT: Thade stalks round Ari, not saying anything. Finally —

THADE
A trade? ... That's what you're proposing. Yourself for the humans ... Even when you were young you took in stray humans. Your family always indulged your every whim.

Thade reaches out — Ari tenses. Thade picks a fleck of dirt from her fur.

THADE (cont'd)
Now look at what you've become.

Ari knows this is her last chance. She has nothing else to offer; so she falls to an ape pose of submissiveness.

ARI
It's what you want, isn't it? I will be with you.

THADE
I have no feelings for you now.

CLOSE ON THADE — He turns his back to her. He takes Ari's SCARF. She watches him drop it into the fire.

CLOSER — in the fire. Thade sees a branding iron. Quickly, Thade spins back and grabs Ari's HAND. Presses the brand into her. Ari cries out.

THADE (cont'd)
You want to be human? ... Then wear their mark.

Thade drops Ari's hand. She runs out as Attar enters.

THADE (cont'd)
Let her return. Tomorrow she will die with the humans.

STAY ON THADE — for one quick moment he looks back for her.

EXT. CALIMA – NIGHT

Leo stands before the ruins giving instructions to his close followers.

LEO
There's one possibility. One shot, but it's worth taking.

He points to the ruins.

LEO (cont'd)
We've got to draw them in close. Put all these people behind the ship. But don't hide them. I want them seen.

DAENA
What about us?

LEO
You'll be on the horseback. In front of the ship. Waiting for my signal. Absolutely still. You're the bait.

BIRN
I won't move till you say so.

LEO
You won't even be out there.

Birn starts to protest, but Leo won't let him.

BIRN
But ...

LEO
That's enough.

INT. CALIMA – THE *OBERON* – BRIDGE

Leo is at the dusty CONTROLS. The MESSENGER box beside him. He's working on something.

Limbo sneaks in as Leo taps the same FUEL GAUGE on the BOARD.

INSERT: Fuel gauge — it flickers and then goes dark. HOLD ON LEO — a moment of doubt plays across his face.

LIMBO
Whatever you're planning ... don't tell me. The anticipation will kill me before Thade does.
(beat, then)
I can't stand it ... you gotta tell me!

LEO
We can't stop them ... but we can scare them. Scramble their monkey minds.

LIMBO
We apes don't scare so easy.

LEO
But when you do ... it's out of control. You start running and never turn back.

EXT. CALIMA THIRD DAY – ON THE CLIFFS – JUST BEFORE DAWN

CLOSE ON LEO: Alone on his horse — at the very edge of the plain. Just watching. For a moment he relives the odyssey that brought him to this moment. Alone with his thoughts.

EXT. CALIMA – LOOKOUT ROCK – NEW ANGLE

Tival as lookout gazing across the plain.

EXT. CALIMA – THADE'S APE ENCAMPMENT – DAWN

CLOSE ON Thade: proud and confident. He finally turns to Attar. Nods.

PUNCH CLOSE on Attar — as he lets out a fearsome *roar*.

EXT. PLAINS OF CALIMA

The APE ARMY stands in crisp formations. The soldiers pick up Attar's roar, echoing it until the sky is filled with their anger. The BUGLERS sound. Thade leads a row of APE RIDERS forward toward CALIMA.

EXT. CALIMA – BEHIND THE RUINS – SAME TIME

The humans are hidden among the ruins. They HEAR the apes before they see them. PAN THE HUMANS'

FACES — as the apes' deep, rolling HOWL breaks over them like a tidal wave. Leo can sense a rising panic among them. He continues to check the controls on his Messenger pack.

NEW ANGLE: There is movement from behind the rocks. Krull and Ari appear. They quickly join the humans.

EXT. CALIMA – LOOKOUT ROCK

ANGLE: TIVAL stands lookout high on the cliff. Calls down.

TIVAL
I see them.

EXT. PLAINS OF CALIMA – ANGLE – MOVING ACROSS THE PLAIN

CLOSER: Thade, Attar and six other horse-mounted apes cantering. He signals — another trumpet call and —

The LOPERS drop from marching to loping position and begin to race forward. They quickly overtake the riders and, passing them, accelerate towards the humans. A sea of red as the ARMY lopes across the plain.

EXT. CALIMA PLAINS

Gunnar, Krull, Daena, and several other riders on their HORSES.

Ari comes riding up. Daena glares at her — until she sees the BRAND on Ari's hand. Ari refuses her pity — moves her horse along the front of the line. As the apes approach, the horses become skittish.

LEO (shouts, re: horses)
Hold them, hold them ... as long as you can.

EXT. CALIMA RUINS – DAY

Gathered humans are hidden among the ruins, watching expectantly. BIRN rides his horse out, moving toward the other horses.

EXT. CALIMA PLAINS – IN FRONT OF THE RUINS – DAY

BACK to the others as Birn rides up.

DAENA
What are you doing here?

BIRN
I'm part of this.

DAENA
Wait with the others like he told you.

But it's too late. The ape LOPERS are too close. Leo gives the signal for the horses to go.

LEO
Now!

THE RIDERS take off at full gallop, heading toward the ruins. They divide into two groups and head for safety behind the ruins.

EXT. CALIMA BEHIND THE RUINS (INTERCUT WITH PLAINS IN FRONT OF THE RUINS)

ON LEO: Watching. Continuing to check his Messenger. He turns to see Birn's horse stumble, pinning Birn underneath.

LEO'S POV: As the ape lopers bear down on Birn.

EXT. CALIMA – IN FRONT OF THE RUINS

ON LEO — He leaps from cover and runs hard into the open across the plain.

ANGLE: The APES explode forward. Birn is directly in their path. Leo runs hard toward him, trying to get to him before Thade does.

BIRN'S POV: The apes bearing down on him.

Leo reaches Birn. He frees Birn's horse, and horse and rider (Birn) gallop out of frame. The apes are closing in. Leo runs full out to get back to the Messenger before he is caught.

EXT. CALIMA PLAINS

QUICK CUT to Thade: watching

from a distance. Unsettled by the sudden silence.

EXT. CALIMA – SIDE OF RUINS

QUICK PAN to Leo: The humans watch Leo's return. He reaches his Messenger just before the apes are upon him.

INSERT: Messenger – as Leo turns it on. No response. Tries again, nothing. Then:

INT. CAVE – THE *OBERON*

QUICK CUT: on the bridge of the *Oberon* — the FUEL MONITOR flickers once, twice, then lights up.

EXT. CALIMA RUINS

WIDE SHOT: The great SPIRES of the ruins are actually the ENGINES of the ship. A LOW HUM radiates from the engines.

EXT. CALIMA RUINS

A beat, then the engines explode to life.

WIDEN: as the rocket thrust EXPLODES.

THEN: The apes in the first row are vaporized. Others behind are burned and tossed into the air.

EXT. CALIMA – THE PLAINS

ON THADE: watching incredulously as his prized warriors tumble burned and scarred into the dust.

PUNCH IN CLOSE on Thade: thinking this over.

EXT. CALIMA RUINS

The engines die out. A giant dust cloud has formed. The few survivors stagger away from the haze.

In the dust and confused panic TWO WOUNDED APE SOLDIERS see humans emerge from the dust and surround them. The apes *growl* — using their tried-and-true instincts to scare the humans away. The humans

growl back. A wild and mocking ROAR that rises from the depths of their souls. It spreads until it drowns out the apes — and their fears. All the humans rush in and begin to beat the surviving apes.

ON LEO WATCHING

EXT. CALIMA — THE PLAINS — THE APE ARMY

Thade and Attar can sense the fear spreading in their troops.

ATTAR
How can there be such a weapon? ... We cannot defeat them.

More wounded stagger back. PUNCH CLOSE on Thade — he listens. The wind whips the dust around them.

INTERCUT: Leo — wondering if he's pulled it off.

LIMBO
It worked! ... I'll gather their weapons and sell them for a fortune!

Leo holds up a hand. Looking out across the plain.

BACK TO THADE: Thade wheels around to Attar.

THADE
We will attack.

ATTAR
But, sir ... he can destroy us all.

Thade draws his sword.

THADE
We will see.

Before Attar can stop him, Thade gallops straight at the humans.

CRANE UP: Thade gallops across the plain.

INTERCUT: Leo steps out from the rocks — all he can see is the dust and haze from the explosion. He listens, too. It's as if he and Thade can sense each other.

Then out of the dust — Thade emerges. Defiant, fearless, riding straight at Calima. He pulls up. Poised, daring them to destroy him.

CLOSE ON LEO — He knows Thade

has played his bluff. Thade flashes his canines and ROARS — it carries across the plain, to ape and human alike.

Limbo can see the look on Leo's face.

LIMBO
By Semos, we're done.

INTERCUT: Thade, as Attar streaks to his side.

THADE
I am tired of this human. Attack!

The HORNS sound. Thade leads the charge into the dust cloud. Attar and the others follow.

EXT. CALIMA — DUST CLOUD

ON LEO: in the thick of battle. ONE APE makes a stab for Leo with a spear — but Leo kicks the spear away. Rolls underneath. Grabs the spear. Sprints forward. Out of the dust another ape soldier appears with a net. Leo grabs a handful of dirt and throws it into the ape's eyes. He stabs him with the spear and takes his net.

EXT. CALIMA – LOOKOUT ROCK

ON THE CLIFF FACE: An ape appears in front of Tival. *Growls.* Tival backs up, bumps into another ape approaching from behind. The two apes toss Tival off the rocks to his death below.

EXT. CALIMA – DUST CLOUD

FIND DAENA: charging through the battle. Fighting valiantly from her horse.

ON THADE: He spots her. With cold resolve he takes a *bola* and swings it over his head. Lets it fly.

Daena is knocked from her mount. She scrambles to her feet. Looks around for help but sees only ape soldiers coming toward her.

EXT. BEHIND THE RUINS – DUST CLOUD

ON ARI: Watching from behind the ruins. She sees Daena's trouble, grabs Birn's horse, mounts it, and rides out to the battle.

EXT. CALIMA – DUST CLOUD

Ari arrives at Daena's side. She reaches down and grabs Daena onto her horse. Their path to safety is blocked by apes.

A mighty ROAR comes from behind. ANGLE — KRULL charges into view, an unstoppable force, wreaking havoc on the ape soldiers who are threatening Ari. They dodge an ape who appears out of the dust. Daena's shoulder is slashed by the ape's spear. Ari holds onto her.

BACK TO KRULL: Surrounded by more ape soldiers. In fierce hand-to-hand combat he crushes several. Then looks up.

EXT. CALIMA

OUT OF THE DUST: ATTAR appears on foot. Both great apes bare their fangs — charge at each other. Locking in a frightening embrace. They cut and slash at each other, first with swords, then with teeth and claws. A blur of fur and dust. At first Krull gains the upper hand. But his age makes him no match for Attar.

EXT. CALIMA – DUST CLOUD

ON LIMBO: Trying to hide from ape soldiers. TWO rush toward him from opposite directions. At the last moment Limbo jumps up, causing the two apes to collide with each other.

INT. CALIMA CAVE – THE *OBERON* – SAME TIME

TRACK IN slowly on the control panel — the red lever — and the Messenger beacon — sounding relentlessly.

CLOSER: On the radar sweep — a blank sweep. Beat. *Then a dot appears.*

EXT. CALIMA – DUST CLOUD

WIDE SHOT: The battle is turning into a rout. Thade charges through looking for Leo.

FIND LEO — he's pulled down from behind. One Ape lifts his sword. INTO FRAME — Limbo runs him through with a spear.

Ari rides back to the human line. Leo and Birn help Daena from the horse. She pushes them away — grabs a weapon and joins the line.

The humans try to retreat to the rocks but the apes have managed to cut off their way. Thade has them surrounded.

EXT. CALIMA – SKY

TILT UP SLIGHTLY — something moves on the horizon. A small glittering dot. Moving too fast to be anything natural.

CLOSER — The "dot" grows in frame.

EXT. CALIMA – DUST CLOUD

Thade wheels his horse and charges at Leo. Leo takes Thade's charge. Thade dismounts, and Leo and Thade begin fierce hand-to-hand combat. Thade quickly gains the upper hand. He swats Leo to the ground. Leo rolls to his feet. Thade lands a crushing blow. Leo falls to one knee. Thade is about to finish him off, stops at a DEAFENING SOUND.

EXT. CALIMA RUINS – ACROSS THE BATTLEFIELD – DUST CLOUD

Apes and humans alike *react* to a sound never heard by anyone on this planet. BOOM! *The breaking of the sound barrier.*

They stop fighting and look up.

IN THE SKY: The "dot" is now rocketing right at them.

Leo fights to clear his mind. *He knows what this is.*

IT'S A POD.

WIDEN: The POD spreads a contrail that filters light into brilliant hues.

All the while we can hear the *beep* of the Messenger beacon.

EXT. CALIMA RUINS

The pod loops back and rockets just above the ground. The wake of the pod disperses the dust cloud. It looks exactly like the parting of the clouds we've seen in the icons of Semos.

Attar watches as the pod skids

through the dirt in a storm of dust and light. The pod finally comes to a stop in front of the ruins.

Thade can't imagine what this means. But he sees that his troops are paralyzed by the sight.

EXT. CALIMA RUINS — ON THE POD

The HATCH OPENS slowly. Inside the pod we can hear the *ping* of the BEACON sounding over and over.

A HAND grips the escape rungs. A furry hand. And PERICLES steps out. The light around him, the swirling of the dust, mimics the icon.

CLOSE ON ATTAR — as he whispers a single word.

ATTAR
Semos.

He drops to his knees.

PAN THE APE SOLDIERS as they think that "Semos" has returned to them. They let out a huge cheer. The same word is repeated over and over among them: "SEMOS."

HOLD ON Thade's reaction — confused and wary.

Attar runs to Thade with eyes wide.

ATTAR (cont'd)
Sir! The prophecy is true. Semos has returned to us.

The humans have no idea what to make of this.

NEW ANGLE: LEO startles them all. He runs to the pod. PERICLES scrambles into Leo's arms. He looks at Leo. Looks down at his hand; picks out a thumb.

CLOSER ON PERICLES: He gives Leo a "thumbs up" sign. Leo returns it.

LEO
Good boy. You brought your pod home.

Now the humans all cheer.

Leo is electrified. Maybe Pericles has brought him a way home, too. Leo slings Pericles' backpack over his own shoulder.

LEO (cont'd)
OK, Pericles, let's go explain evolution to the monkeys.

ON THADE: watching his soldiers throw down their weapons as Leo strides toward them. Thade rushes at his soldiers.

THADE
Stop him! ...

Thade pushes a few toward Leo. These apes drop their weapons, too, and retreat. Thade tries to stop them.

THADE (cont'd)
Go back ... I order you ... hold your positions ... cowards!

The humans cheer as they see the apes flee. It's a day they thought they'd never see.

Attar watches his soldiers scatter. Confused, not sure what to do.

Thade *growls* — then charges and LEAPS — landing hard on Leo. With one vicious backhand he sends Pericles sprawling into the dust. Attar and the other apes are shocked.

THADE (cont'd) (to Leo)
Wherever you come from ... you're still just a wretched human.

Thade grabs Leo and hurls him through the air. Leo hits the ground hard. Pericles' backpack skitters along the rocks. Leo looks at Thade and runs for it. Thade charges Leo and throws him again. Leo takes another terrible fall.

CLOSE ON LEO: as he pushes himself up out of the dust. He can see the backpack laying by the ENTRANCE to the *Oberon*. He gets to his feet and stands defiantly. Thade is enraged.

Leo retreats — luring Thade closer to the *Oberon*'s bridge.

Thade lopes forward and swats Leo back again. Leo lands by the backpack — tries furtively to reach into it before Thade can see. But Thade is on him too fast. Leo staggers back — Thade charges and follows him INTO THE TUNNEL.

INT. CALIMA CAVE — *OBERON* TUNNEL

Thade slaps Leo again — and Leo tumbles deeper into the *Oberon*.

INT. CALIMA CAVE — THE *OBERON* TUNNEL

Leo staggers down the old cave.

INT. CALIMA CAVE — *OBERON*

Thade throws Leo through the SECURITY DOOR onto the BRIDGE.

ON THE BRIDGE — Thade and Leo: Thade stands over Leo. Looking around at this strange place.

THADE
I will bury your remains ... so they can be forgotten like the rest of your race.

Thade starts for Leo — but Leo manages to reach into Pericles' backpack and pull out the standard issue GUN.

He wheels on Thade. Thade stops immediately.

LEO (*reacting*)
You know what this is.

Thade does. He is stunned. Caught off guard. Everything has turned around so quickly ... until —

ONTO THE BRIDGE: Ari rushes in looking for Leo, but finds —

THADE — who leaps on her so quickly Leo dare not shoot. Thade stands with one hand gripping Ari's throat tightly. Leo points the gun at Thade.

LEO (cont'd)
Let her go.

THADE
I'm willing to die. ... Are you willing to see her die?

Leo realizes he has no option. He sets down the gun. KICKS it to Thade. It spins on the hard surface. INTO FRAME — ATTAR — appears on the bridge. Picks up the gun. Holds it up as if he can't trust his eyes.

THADE (cont'd) (to Attar)
With that weapon they are no longer the weaker race. We can't allow it.

Leo speaks quickly to Attar.

LEO (re: ship)
Look around ... this is who you really are. We brought you here. We lived together with you in peace ... until Semos murdered everyone.

ATTAR
No ... (turns to Thade)
Can it be true?

THADE
They'd make us their slaves ...
Bring me the gun.

Attar is confused. He finally presents it to Thade. Thade shoves Ari to the floor. Takes the gun. Thade lets his long finger wrap around the gun's trigger.

THADE (cont'd)
Does it really make a difference how we arrived here? We are the only ones who will survive.

Ari pleads with Thade.

ARI
Please don't hurt him.

Thade *reacts*, looks at Ari.

THADE
I was always less than human to you. (points the gun) Someday if humans are even remembered, they will be known for what they really are ... weak and stupid ...

Thade PULLS THE TRIGGER. Nothing happens. He pulls it over and over.

LEO
Stupid people, smart guns.

Thade turns to Attar.

THADE
Kill them.

CLOSE ON ATTAR — He doesn't move.

THADE (cont'd)
I'm your commander. Obey me.

ATTAR
Everything I have believed in ... is a lie. You and your family have betrayed us. I will not follow you anymore.

CLOSER — Leo is maneuvering Thade to one side of the bridge, away from Ari and Attar.

THADE
When you're dead and this place is buried beneath the rocks ... no one will know the truth.

Leo takes one more step aside.

LEO
You will ... forever.

Leo presses his hand to the WALL. Thade doesn't understand what he's doing until —

INT. CALIMA CAVE — THE BRIDGE — CONTINUOUS

The glass SECURITY DOOR of the *Oberon* begins to slide shut.

Leo grabs Ari and pulls her out.

Thade is taken by surprise. Confused at first. Then with all his great power he grips the door as it closes.

CLOSE ON Thade's hands: With a terrifying roar Thade struggles and begins to slide the DOOR back.

INTO FRAME — another, larger set of hands: gripping Thade's wrists. Thade looks up to see —

ATTAR – staring calmly, firmly at him.

THADE
Help me ... my friend ...
(then)
... I command you ...

ATTAR
I will pray for you.

Attar forcefully throws Thade back. THE DOOR LOCKS CLOSED.

WIDEN: Thade slams himself into the DOOR. Over and over. But this glass

is beyond even an ape's force. Attar just stares at Thade. Then turns and walks away.

ON THADE — through the glass. Beats on the door viciously. But they can no longer hear the sound of his *roars*.

Thade runs to the CONTROL PANEL. Starts to pound the board. His strength has no effect on the sophisticated technology.

ECU: Thade slams his hands down on the buttons. He is trapped.

ANGLE: Leo turns to look for Pericles. But he's gone. Ari kneels down, touches a BLOOD TRAIL that leads Leo to —

INT. CALIMA CAVE/*OBERON* – ANIMAL LIVING QUARTERS

Leo comes into the "cave" that was once the animal laboratory of the *Oberon*.

Pericles climbs slowly into the hole that was once his cage. The only home he's ever known.

CLOSER: Pericles curls in the corner and lays his head down. Breathing softly.

INTO FRAME: Leo takes his hand. Smiles at him.

DISSOLVE TO: EXT. PLAINS OF CALIMA – DAY

Wind sweeps across the battlefield.

AT THE RUINS: FIND Attar kneeling at KRULL'S GRAVE. Attar places a last stone on top.

INTO FRAME: Ari touches Krull's grave.

ARI
All the years you put up with me ... this time I wish I could have protected you.

WIDEN: Leo comes INTO FRAME with Pericles. Hands him to Ari.

LEO
Take good care of him.

ARI
I can promise you I won't put him in a cage.

Attar looks across the battlefield.

ATTAR
We will leave the graves unmarked. No one who comes here will be able to tell ape from human. They will be mourned together ... as it should be from now on.

INSERT: POD, as a loud *beeping* starts.

BACK TO LEO: reacting to the sound.

LEO
It's found the coordinates of the storm that brought me here.

Ari is trying to contain her emotions.

ARI
It would mean a great deal to everyone if you would stay ...
(then)

It would mean a great deal to me ...

Leo's mind is already made up. The BEEPING continues.

LEO
I have to leave now ... I have to take a chance that it can get me back.

Ari touches Leo in a gentle, grooming manner. There is heartbreak in her voice. Ari starts to say something, nods.

ARI
One day they'll tell a story about a human who came from the stars and changed our world. ... Some will say it was just a fairy tale ... that he was never real ...

Ari's eyes well up.

ARI (cont'd)
... but I'll know the truth.

The BEEPING increases frequency. Leo backs up and then starts sprinting for the pod.

EXT. THE POD (CONTINUOUS)

Leo comes running up. Surprising LIMBO coming out. Limbo immediately turns around — tries to hide something behind his back. Looks at Leo. Then sighs — Limbo holds out an *OBERON* EMBLEM.

LEO
You gonna sell that?

LIMBO (sincerely)
No ... I wanted something to remember you by.

He holds it out to Leo. Leo presses it back into his hand.

LEO
Make sure you get a good price.

OFF TO THE SIDE — DAENA tries to stand proudly. Leo goes to her. She finally breaks down — wraps her arms around him and holds him tight.

LEO (cont'd)
You know I can't take you with me ...

DAENA
Then you'll have to come back.

She kisses him deeply. Then runs off.

CIRCLE ROUND Leo as he takes one last look around at the PLANET and climbs into the POD.

INT. POD

Leo slips on his helmet.

LEO
Close pod.

The HATCH slides closed.

WIDEN: EXT. CALIMA – DAY

Ari, Daena, Attar, Limbo, and the others shield their eyes as the POD rises in the sky.

WIDE SHOT — SKY

Birn sits alone on horseback at the top of the cliffs as a STREAK OF LIGHT blazes across the sky. Ascending until the bright light disappears.

INT. ALPHA POD – LATER

The perfect blackness of space. Leo is trying to map his coordinates.

His control panel lights up: A message reads:

COORDINATES UNKNOWN

WIDEN SHOT: The same rush of LIGHTS we saw from the ELECTRO-MAGNETIC STORM appears to Leo's right. Blinding him — as it did before.

The Alpha pod is suddenly overwhelmed with light from the worm hole. And then it DISAPPEARS.

FELLOW HUMANS

The story doesn't end here, but the
final scenes of *Planet of the Apes*
were kept secret at the time this
book went to press.

Future editions will contain the
final ending. Meanwhile, enjoy
the film in theaters and visit
www.planetoftheapes.com
for more details.

TWENTIETH CENTURY FOX Presents

A ZANUCK COMPANY Production

A TIM BURTON FILM

MARK WAHLBERG
TIM ROTH
HELENA BONHAM CARTER

MICHAEL CLARKE DUNCAN
KRIS KRISTOFFERSON
ESTELLA WARREN
PAUL GIAMATTI
CARY-HIROYUKI TAGAWA
DAVID WARNER

Special Make-up Effects Designed and Created by
RICK BAKER

Special Animation and Visual Effects by
INDUSTRIAL LIGHT & MAGIC

Music by
DANNY ELFMAN

Costume Designer
COLLEEN ATWOOD

Film Editor
CHRIS LEBENZON, A.C.E.

Production Designer
RICK HEINRICHS

Director of Photography
PHILIPPE ROUSSELOT, AFC/ASC

Executive Producer
RALPH WINTER

Produced by
RICHARD D. ZANUCK

Screenplay by
WILLIAM BROYLES, JR. and LAWRENCE KONNER & MARK D. ROSENTHAL

Directed by
TIM BURTON

acknowledgments

Newmarket Press wishes to thank the following for their special contributions to this book:

At Twentieth Century Fox: Jim Gianopulos, Chairman Fox Filmed Entertainment; Tom Rothman, Chairman Fox Filmed Entertainment; Lisa Licht, Senior Vice President of Marketing; photo editor Melissa Duke, archivist Karen Hernandez, Jennifer Robinson, and especially Debbie Olshan in Fox Consumer Products for attentively shepherding the project through.

Executive producer Ralph Winter and David Gorder in the *Planet of the Apes* production office, who provided invaluable assistance; unit publicist Eileen Peterson; and visual effects producer Tom Peitzman.

Derek Frey, assistant to Tim Burton.

Mr. Charlton Heston, his representative, Jack Gilardi, and publicist Lisa Powers, for their cooperation and assistance.

Unit photographers Sam Emerson and David James; production artists Mauro Borelli, Matt Codd, Sylvain Despretz, Guy Hendrix Dyas, and James Oxford; and storyboard artist Michael Jackson.

Production designer Rick Heinrichs, costume designer Colleen Atwood, makeup designer Rick Baker and Heidi Holicker of Cinovation, for providing additional illustrations.

Stephen Kenneally, Miles Perkinson, and Ellen Pasternack at Industrial Light & Magic.

Contributing writer Mark Salisbury for his insightful coverage of the filmmaking process.

Book designer Timothy Shaner and Christopher Measom of Night & Day Design; editor Diana Landau of Parlandau Communications; and Esther Margolis, Keith Hollaman, Frank DeMaio, Tom Perry and Kelli Taylor at Newmarket Press.

Our deepest thanks go to director Tim Burton and producer Richard D. Zanuck, for their passionate vision in creating *Planet of the Apes* and their generous contributions to this book about it.